THE IRON WAR
2E7-2E11

KELSON HAYES

THE IRON WAR

PRINTED BY AMAZON

FIRST EDITION/ 2019

ALL RIGHTS RESERVED

©2019 by Kelson Clarke Hayes

FRONTCOVER DESIGN BY AMAZON

THE COPYWRITTEN PORTIONS OF THIS BOOK MAY NOT BE REPRODUCED OR TRANSMITTED IN ANY FORM OR BY ANY MEANS, ELECTRONIC OR MECHANICAL, INCLUDING PHOTOCOPYING, RECORDING, OR BY ANY INFORMATION STORAGE AND RETRIEVAL SYSTEM, WITHOUT THE EXPRESS PERMISSION OF THE AUTHOR, EXCEPT WHERE PERMITTED BY LAW.

If you purchased this book without a cover you should be aware that this book is stolen property. It is reported as "unsold and destroyed" to the publisher, and neither the author nor the publisher has received any payment for this "stripped book".

Manufactured in the United States of America.

TABLE OF CONTENTS

CHAPTER	PAGE
TABLE OF CONTENTS	
MAP OF SOUTHEAST AERBON	
MAP OF VOSKA	
MAP OF AERBON	
PROLOGUE	p.1
CHAPTER ONE	p.2
CHAPTER TWO	p.7
CHAPTER THREE	p.12
CHAPTER FOUR	p.17
CHAPTER FIVE	p.21
CHAPTER SIX	p.25
CHAPTER SEVEN	p.29
CHAPTER EIGHT	p.35
CHAPTER NINE	p.42
CHAPTER TEN	p.47
CHAPTER ELEVEN	p.51
CHAPTER TWELVE	p.56
CHAPTER THIRTEEN	p.60
CHAPTER FOURTEEN	p.64
CHAPTER FIFTEEN	p.69
CHAPTER SIXTEEN	p.73
CHAPTER SEVENTEEN	p.76
CHAPTER EIGHTEEN	p.79
CHAPTER NINETEEN	p.84
CHAPTER TWENTY	p.89
CHAPTER TWENTY-ONE	p.92

CHAPTER TWENTY-TWO	p.96
CHAPTER TWENTY-THREE	p.100
CHAPTER TWENTY-FOUR	p.103
CHAPTER TWENTY-FIVE	p.108
CHAPTER TWENTY-SIX	p.111
CHAPTER TWENTY-SEVEN	p.115
CHAPTER TWENTY-EIGHT	p.118
CHAPTER TWENTY-NINE	p.121
CHAPTER THIRTY	p.125
CHAPTER THIRTY-ONE	p.128
CHAPTER THIRTY-TWO	p.131
CHAPTER THIRTY-THREE	p.134
CHAPTER THIRTY-FOUR	p.137
CHAPTER THIRTY-FIVE	p.141
CHAPTER THIRTY-SIX	p.143
CHAPTER THIRTY-SEVEN	p.146
CHAPTER THIRTY-EIGHT	p.150
CHAPTER THIRTY-NINE	p.153
CHAPTER FORTY	p.156
CHAPTER FORTY-ONE	p.159
EPILOGUE	p.163
FIREARMS	p.165
TERRITORIAL MAP OF SOUTHEAST AERBON	p.167

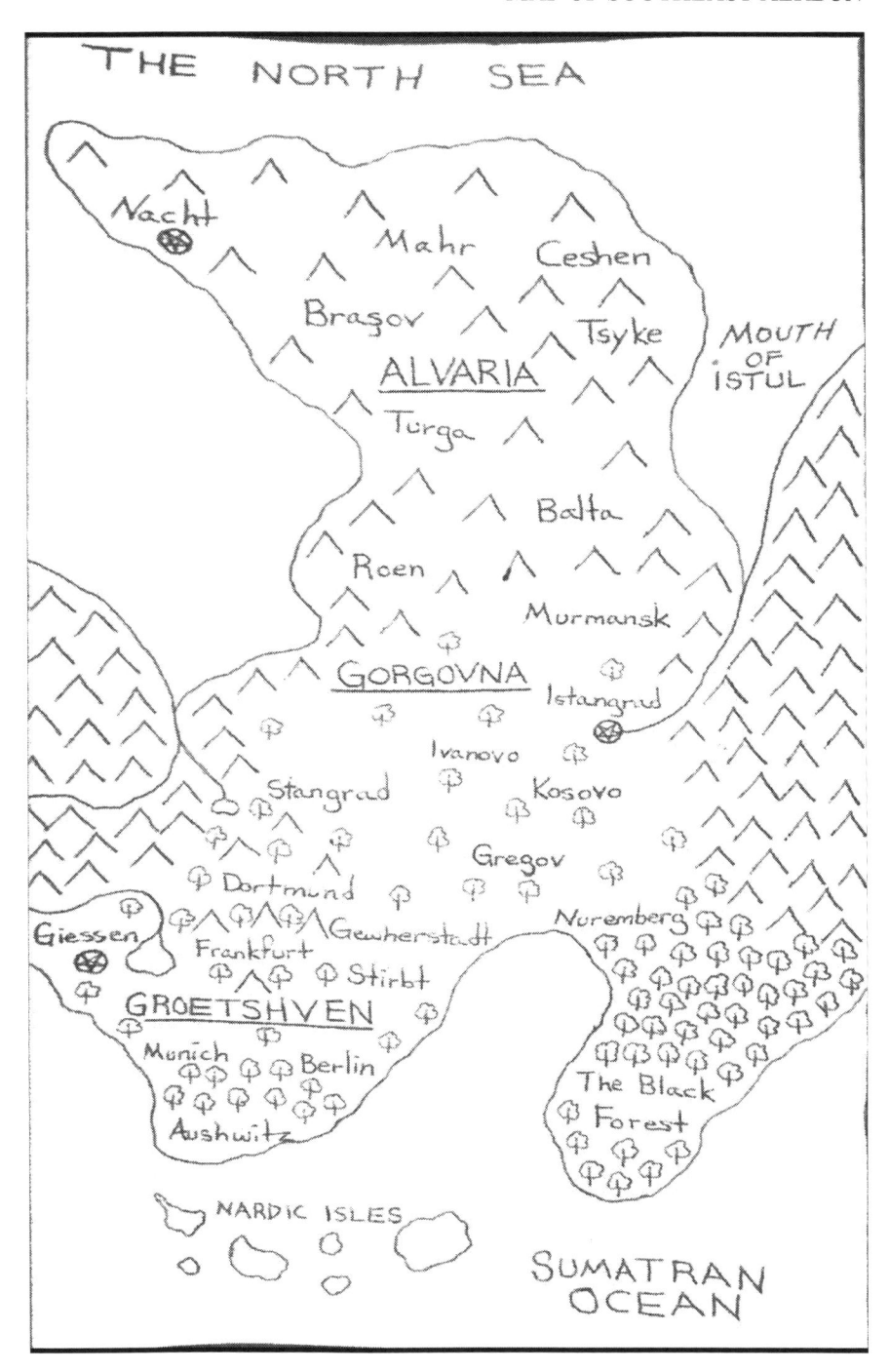

MAP OF SOUTHEAST AERBON

MAP OF VOSKA

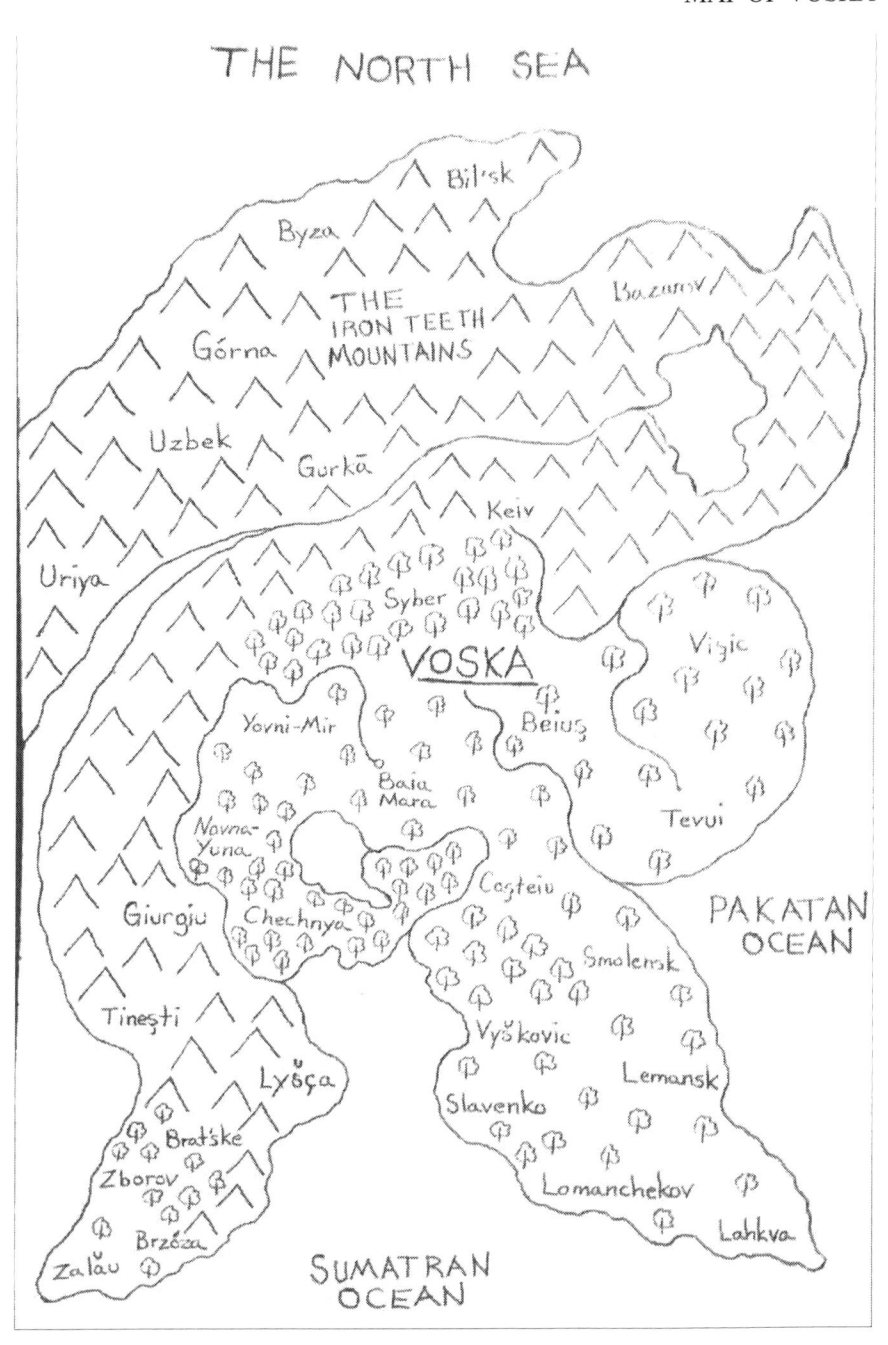

MAP OF AERBON

PROLOGUE

Serving under Dmitri Porfiry Yaroslavovich, the Iron Highway's construction was successfully completed by the Voskan Army in the Winter of 1E199. It created a means of travel between Voska and Aerbon via the inhospitable Iron Teeth Mountains by means of a 1175km highway; of which 563km consisted of underground tunnels that cut through the very mountains themselves. Upon their discovery of the Gorgon lands that comprised the majority of eastern Aerbon, the Voskan Army eradicated what was left of the fleeing orcish troops as well as the invading vampiric legions. Armed with muskets and primitive grenades, they wiped out the monstrous creatures that threatened to engulf the surviving veterans of The Gorgon War who took refuge in the former orcish capitol of Istul. First Marshal Dmitri Porfiry Yaroslavovich of the Voskan Army introduced himself to Captain Vasil, the commander of Gilan's army as well as Captain of the First Swordsman Company, and claimed the new-found land in the name of Vladyslav Vladimirovich-Ivanovna; the Tsar of the Voskan Republic.

Though there was some disagreement on the part of the elves of Gilan and the remnants of the Nardic tribesmen, they inevitably yielded to the superiority of the Voskan Army, following Dmitri's orders to depart from that place at once. Meanwhile in Gilan, the elvish kingdom was taken by surprise after the Great Chieftain of the Nardic Tribes sent forth the full strength of his army to seize Gilan by storm in what they called a blitzkrieg, or "lightning war". They took the kingdom in its vulnerable state in the midst of the Gorgon campaign and claimed the land for themselves, uniting the Nardic Tribes and calling their nation the Confederation of Groetshven; a country comprised of independent city-states united under the autonomous rule of the acting Kaiser of the Confederacy.

CHAPTER ONE

GEWEHRSTADT, GROETSHVEN

Spring, 2E8

It was a warm spring day in the town of Gewehrstadt and Tobias Schumacher roamed the hilly wooded countryside on the outskirts of the town. He'd moved there with his mother in the Summer of 2E5 to be reunited with his father following the Fall of Gilan and the unification of the Confederate State of Groetshven. That was nearly three years ago and now Tobias was the ripe age of fifteen. He spent most of his time roaming the countryside and painting, dedicating himself to finding the most beautiful landscapes and scenes in nature to transfer to a canvas with his handy paintbrush. Occasionally Tobias would sell his paintings for small amounts of silver, though his father was insistent that he follow in his footsteps as a cobbler. His father Klaus had served as a soldier in the days before the Groetshven Confederacy when they were known as the Nardic Tribes, though after the Gorgon War and the Fall of Gilan he'd retired from military service and took up work as a cobbler.

His job primarily revolved around crafting boots for the soldiers and factory workers that inhabited the small town, best known for being Groetshven's largest producer of muskets. Gewehrstadt, which literally translates to "Gun Town" in the Nardic Tongue, had a population of roughly 14,000 with the majority of its residents taking up employment in the musket factory that took up the entire northwest portion of the town. There were a couple of schools and some local businesses that supplied the townsfolk with the necessary essentials as well as police and firemen to keep them safe and maintain order. Life was rather pleasant and peaceful in Gewehrstadt, interrupted only by the occasional crack of gunfire that erupted from the hunters in their pursuit of the elk that inhabited those heavily wooded lands. Tobias wasn't worried about the hunters as they wouldn't be much of a presence in those parts until Autumn when the elk were in season and so it was that he preoccupied himself with trying to find the perfect viewpoint to paint one of his majestic landscapes.

The natural countryside surrounding the town was beautiful and and bountiful with life; squirrels darted across from tree to tree whilst birds sang their songs in the boughs above between their short bursts of flight. Tobias continued to make his way along the winding woodland path that he followed, enjoying the cool breeze that weaved through the dense populace of birch trees to cool down the woodland creatures residing under the shade of those magnificent trees. His father had told him stories of the elves that once lived in those lands before the orcs had wiped their people out of existence, prior to the conclusion of the Gorgon War. Tobias had asked his father of the war a few times since they'd moved from their home on Dusseldorf to the mainland confederate state, though Klaus Schumacher didn't have much to say on the matter.

"It was a dark and terrible time Tobias; you can't imagine the horrors of war or the death and bloodshed we bore witness to." his father would say in response to the question, *"We came here and took the lands back from the evil creatures that seized them and we fought off the Voskan invaders, what more is there to say?"*

Turning his attention back to the present, Tobias plopped himself upon the ground and went about setting up his canvas stand and paints. He'd stumbled upon a natural embankment where River Gianor cut through the wooded lands curving on a more south-westerly route where it headed towards Giessen; the capitol of the Confederate State of Groetshven. There were some elk drinking from the river on the other side of the bank and birds resting in the boughs of the trees nearby singing in unison, creating a peaceful atmosphere for the young painter. He busied himself about replicating the scene on his canvas sheet and lost himself for hours in the endeavour. Painting away, he turned the blank sheet from an empty expanse of white into a window that showed his world the way he saw it and he poured his whole heart and soul into it. Once the scene was completed he packed his things and departed, making the trek back home before the sun set for the day.

"Ah, so you're finally back! Where have you been, painting again? Your father has been looking for you, you know." his mother greeted him as Tobias entered the house.

"*Wie gehts Mutter?*" Tobias inquired rather nonchalantly.

"*Wie gehts?*" his mother replied incredulously, "Why don't you go find your father in his shop and see for yourself; it seemed to be rather important to him that he speak with you."

Tobias appeased his mother, stating that he would put up his things in his room and set out immediately to find his father in town. His father's shop was situated in the heart of the town centre about half an hour's walk away from the house and Tobias made the trek without event. It was a warm spring day and everyone in town was too busy enjoying the weather to bother Tobias on his stroll. Dodging some porters in the streets, Tobias pushed through the bustle as the beautifully-wrought blue sign for his father's shop loomed on the horizon over the heads of the crowd. Making his way through the door into the store, the youth approached the till and called out for his father who appeared shortly thereafter.

"*Guten tag*, my son; it is good to finally see you. I take it your mother sent you?" Klaus greeted his son, setting down the leather shoe he'd been preoccupied with repairing.

"*Ja*; she said you wanted to speak with me." Tobias replied, rather skeptically.

"Ah, yes. Take a seat Tobias." his father said, motioning to one of the chairs designated for his customers and clients.

"You'll be turning sixteen soon and it will be time to start thinking of a profession; I want you to come with me to the shop and take up cobbling. It is a good trade, and honest. Your mother and I think it is time." Klaus continued once Tobias had seated himself, though the young lad quickly rose back to his feet in protest.

"But father, I've been selling my paintings in the town and saving money; I want to be a painter and travel the world and share it with everyone! I've just been waiting until my birthday to ask your blessing." Tobias exclaimed.

"You'll starve and die, either in the wilderness or in the streets. Painting is a hobby and you need to take up a real job if you want to have a life for yourself. Even being a soldier is better than being a painter, but I can teach you how to be a cobbler. You can carry on the tradition of our family." his father snapped back.

"What tradition? You're just a soldier-turned-cobbler; you know nothing of the world! All you know is death, killing, and shoes!" Tobias shot back before turning away and leaving.

"If you want to leave so badly then you can just pack your things and go!" Klaus shouted after his now-disowned son.

CHAPTER TWO

GREGOV, GORGOVNA

Winter, 2E8

Aleksy Zuykov Ilyich was formerly a peasant from the town of Tineşti where he struggled to get by as a farmer with his wife and two sons. The town was divided into communities by the noblemen that owned the serfs and free peasants that lived off the land. The indentured serfs lived in communal estates built on the land owned by the three Boyars that shared ownership of the town; having divvied up the township between themselves, they sold portions of the lands to the local free men and peasants that inhabited the surrounding region. Aleksy was separated from his family in 1E192 at the ripe age of 24 for national service. He served under one of First Marshall Dmitri Porfiry Yaroslavovich's many underlings during the construction of The Iron Highway primarily as a labourer, though he was armed and outfitted as a soldier of the Voskan Army.

He fought alongside his fellow countrymen, repelling a vampiric onslaught as they colonised the newfoundland beyond the inhospitable westernmost reaches of the cruel and unforgiving Iron Teeth Mountains. Sixteen years had passed since the day he'd been separated from his family and still he served under the Voskan Army in those lands, awaiting the day he could retire and return home to his family as a free man. He would receive a payment of Я1,500* as his retirement along with his freedom upon serving the mandatory minimum of 10 years servitude, with a maximum of 20 years of

---

*The Rinska was the common unit of currency in Voska, established originally in 1E78 during the rule of Vladimirovich Vladyslava Ivanovna; son of Vladimir Ivanovna: the founder of Voska.

service in exchange for a retirement payout of Я5,000. Unfortunately, due to disciplinary action, his mandatory duty had been extended to a minimum of 18 years of service, of which he still had two years to go. His time was nearly up and Aleksy had spent the majority of it plotting out what he would do upon receiving his freedom; having set his sights on following through with a solid 20 years of service in exchange for the maximum payout. He often fantasized of buying his own plot of land and spending the short remainder of his life with his wife, Dunia, and his two sons; living off the land and passing it down to the eldest son whilst giving the monetary inheritance to the younger son when the time inevitably came.

His sons, Alexei and Petyr Ilyich, were 20 and 17 years old; Alexei had just reached the minimum age of eligibility for selection into national service and his mother was worried for him. She wrote to her husband regularly over the years and they'd maintained consistent communication via post. In the last letter she wrote on Alexei's twentieth birthday, she told her husband of the growing discontent back home in Tineşti; it was rumoured that the Voskan Army was starting to make moves to muster more troops across the country. Upon completion of the Iron Highway in 1E199, a second draft had been enacted, though their boys had been too young to serve in those days. Now however, there were rumours that yet another draft would soon spread across the nation, sweeping through the cities, town, and villages like a murder of carrion crows.

Aleksy worried for his sons; the Voskan Army made national service a mandatory requirement of all men between the age of 20-25 and the minimum requirement was 5 years, though in the event of a mandatory draft all selected draftees were required to do a minimum of 10 years. The required time of service could also be extended as a result of disciplinary action or simply because a commanding officer didn't like a particular soldier or wanted to hold onto an exceptional one. For those reasons Aleksy feared for his sons' futures, as well as his wife's. Petyr was still too young to be selected for duty, though it wasn't certain when the draft would be enacted if there was any truth to the rumours. Though Aleksy hoped that neither of his sons would be snatched away from their homestead, his mind also drifted to the subconscious fears for his wife's well-being.

They were both beginning to feel their age creep up on them and she couldn't take care of all the duties of the estate on her own. Until he could retire from the military and buy their freedom from the Boyar that owned them, Aleksy and his family were the property of Nikolai Koval Surikov. The Boyar's brother, Vasiliy, was a notorious alcoholic and womaniser with countless accusations of rape and sexual assault against him from the peasantry, even amongst the children. Being of nobility, Vasiliy was above the law and quite often found himself taking blatant advantage of the fact. Those he couldn't intimidate with his social standing he bought off with his money and so he never found himself in much trouble for very long at all, though his brother often berated him and was often found publicly shaming and humiliating him for his lecherous, perverted, and consumptuous ways.

Aleksy did not like being so far from his wife and unable to protect her from such situations, though there was little he could do to prevent it even had he been around. Floggings were all too common a punishment for the peasantry and besides; Dunia was fully capable of handling her own against the wretched man. He hadn't expressed any interest in her for nearly twelve years; she had made her feelings towards the abominable drunk quite clear after rejecting his advances by breaking several of Vasiliy's toes with a swift stomp of her foot. She was entirely capable of defending herself, but still; Aleksy loved his wife and so he worried for her as well as his sons. Shaking himself out of his thoughtful reverie, the Voskan peasant-soldier brought himself back to the present; it was his turn at watch duties and everything was dead silent and still in that late hour of the night.

"*Privet*, my friend; lost in thought?" Josef chuckled, pouring himself a glass of vodka and pouring a second for his friend.

Aleksy laughed and shook it off, telling his fellow soldier of the watch that he'd just been starting to nod off, accepting the vodka that would help to renew his vigour. They drank a couple rounds and took long drags on their pipes, chatting between themselves of the Voskan current events and politics and exchanging tales of their hometowns. The pair were both from the more mountainous southwestern farming region; Josef's hometown of Lyšça was very similar to Aleksy own hometown in many ways and the two bonded over it. They had both been farmers in their former lives as peasants, primarily growing tuber plants such as potatoes, turnips, and beets and growing barely enough to get by after the local Boyar had deducted his taxable share of the crops.

So it was that they laughed and made jokes about the system they lived under, relating to one another and enjoying the semi-pessimistic camaraderie that they shared. They saw the flaws of the world in which they lived and accepted them as the immutable facts of life that they were, choosing instead to laugh about them together rather than dwell on it in a constant state of hopelessness. Josef poured a third round and Aleksy declared it to be his last, feeling the first two starting to creep up on him. Even as Josef teased him jokingly, the pair continued in their mirth and downed the drinks, taking a break to smoke their pipes as they attempted to regain their senses momentarily. A shot cracked off and startled the pair out of their routine night of watch duty, whizzing just inches from where Josef's had had been moments ago prior to leaning back to exhale the drag he'd just taken from his pipe…

CHAPTER THREE

GIESSEN, GROETSHVEN

Autumn, 2E8

Though the weather was still fair in the southern lands of the Groetshven Confederacy, it was beginning to get cooler as the days simultaneously grew shorter. Summer had given way to Autumn and soon it would be Winter; nearly six months had passed since Tobias ran away from his family's home and now he found himself living in the capitol - barely getting by as a painter, though he was happy. He rented a small room in a destitute-looking tavern on the outskirts of the massive city. The city centre was constructed entirely out of marble and there was a beautiful castle built by the elves in the heart of it, though the Nardic Army had gone about expanding the city by contributing their own constructs around the original elvish capitol. Tobias took advantage of this and used the beautiful setting as a source of inspiration for his painting and made a living by selling the art to visitors of the town or the occasional random passerby in the street.

Construction and labour were the two main fields of work that dominated the capitol as the Groetshven Confederacy was focused predominantly on production and expansion, being in its early stages of foundation as a nation. The industrial revolution had blew up in Giessen and there was an over-wealth of factories throughout the city. Production was booming and it was notably one of the richest cities in Aerbon at the time; they exported their goods throughout Aerbon via their own merchant navy, removing the need for the Roman middlemen that plagued the elves of Gilan during their reign in the First Era prior to the Nardic *blitzkrieg*. Tobias had no interest in the fields of construction, labour, or factory work and so he stuck to selling his paintings in the streets. He mostly busked around the high street and the market district when he wasn't preoccupied with painting in the streets finding the most beautiful views he could throughout the city. Occasionally people would stop and observe him in the midst of his painting and place him an offer upon his completion, though there were more often than not periods that he went days at a time without a single sale, though he never faltered or despaired for even a second in his passion.

In the six months that had passed since he'd run away his mother had written to him twice by post after receiving the first letter from her soon a little over two months ago. He told her that he was faring well as an artist and that he would start sending her and his father money soon enough when he was rich. She replied that he should save his money and never forget where he came from and told him that she loved him dearly. In her last letter to him, she warned Tobias that the soldiers had passed through town enlisting the local vagabonds* into military service and that they had been looking for him. His father told the soldiers that Tobias had run away to become an artist and that he hadn't heard from the lad since. He suggested that his son was dead, having most likely starved to death, though he doubted they would ever be certain. His mother warned that they would probably still be on the lookout for him and gave her love, suggesting that he cease contact lest his father catch wind of it and report him for duty.

---

*Anyone aged 16-20 years of age and unemployed or not presently under apprenticeship/enlistment was eligible for four years of mandatory national service.

Tobias did his best to follow his mother's advice, trying to keep a low profile between his travels. He'd been residing in Giessen for nearly three months after traversing between the numerous city-states that comprised the Confederacy. Recently however, the Groetshven Confederation had secured an alliance with the Roman Empire, promising their new allies muskets and aid to wage war against the neighbouring nation of Itania to the west of the River Rome that split their peninsula. Along with open borders between both nations, the alliance also decreed that both sides would offer at least one third of their total military forces to aid the other in their active war campaigns. Rome was busy at work plotting out their conquest of Itania whilst Groetshven already had its sights set on Voska and the Gorgon lands, or Gorgovna as the Voskan people called the place.

This recent news had inspired Tobias to pack up his things and move and so he had gone about starting the process, though he still had some things he had to sell lest he end up throwing away or leaving behind countless paintings to be lost and forgotten by time. He was planning on taking a caravan west sometime around the end of the week, taking with him all that he could carry on his travels. He was thinking of escaping to the city-centre of the capitol in the heart of the Roman Empire, having heard in Giessen of the luxurious city's beauty. He had already selected and set aside the seven Groetshven paintings that he would take with him to sell in Rome as a sort of souvenir item from their eastern neighbour. In the meantime, he continued to busk in the streets of Giessen where he continued to rent his room for the time being until the inevitable day of his move.

"You're quite talented young man; how much for the painting?" an older gentleman stopped in the street to remark on the picture Tobias busied himself about painting.

"Ah, *vielen danke*; for you I will sell it for five silver pieces." Tobias replied, to which the man was agreeable. Upon receiving his payment for the piece, Tobias quickly finished it and gave it to the man before packing up for the day. He still had nine paintings sitting in his flat though he figured that he would just take the two extras along with him; there wasn't much of a difference between 7 and 9 canvases in addition to a sack of clothes and painting supplies anyhow.

Purchasing himself a ticket to Rome from a nearby caravan company in the city centre on the way home, Tobias packed up the handful of things he kept in the flat and made ready for his adventure. Upon hoisting his sackcloth pack over his shoulder and grabbing his prized collection of paintings, he paid off the remainder of his rent fees and turned in his room key to the landlord. Having all of his affairs in order and everything finalised he made for the caravan's boarding station where they would be departing that evening, giving him some time to sell a couple paintings. He sold three pieces during his time there and bought himself a meal and a pint for five copper coins. Shortly after finishing his supper they began the boarding process in preparation for the wagon's departure and so he loaded up his things and joined the queue.

The wagon could hold a total of eight passengers along with the two drivers that drove the horse-drawn carriage. The caravan was comprised of three such wagon, though only two were bound for the Roman capitol. The other was bound for Gewehrstadt, making a stop in Auschwitz along the way as one of the boarding officials announced. Tobias seated himself at the window and before long they departed from the station and rode along the high street on their way out of town. The wooded Groetshven countryside passed them by on their westward journey and before long they were passing through the Feiro Forest as they followed the River Gianor over the Groetshven border and into the Roman Empire. Passing through the town of Feiro, the caravan eventually made a stop in Ceivos where two of the wagon's occupants disembarked, having reached their destination. The caravan took a break for the night and an announcement was made that they would resume their travels in the morning, advising the passengers to seek out accommodations in the town centre.

CHAPTER FOUR

TINEȘTI, VOSKA

Spring, 2E9

"We are looking for Alexei Rodionovna Ilyich." a burly Voskan officer greeted Dunia at her door with ten soldiers at his back outfitted in the Voskan Army's standard-issued uniform; a bland tan overcoat with the red insignia of the Voskan state.

"No! No… You can't do this, not again! First you people take my husband and now you come for my sons one by one until I am no more than a childless widow." Dunia attempted to brush the group of men away as she sought to slam the door shut in their faces, though the officer's hand was too quick.

"*Cyka blyat!* You think you can stop the Voskan Army?" the officer spat as he cursed her, forcing the door open and pushing her aside as he made room for his men to storm the house.

"Alexei, Petyr; run!" Dunia shrieked as she sank to her knees from the overwhelming stress, terror, and hopelessness that consumed her. She could hear the sounds of shock, fear, and confusion that erupted from her sons as the pair peeled off, sprinting away from their family's farmstead towards the treeline of woods that encompassed the mountainous lands to the north of Tineşti. Despite their best efforts, the brothers were quickly apprehended by the Voskan soldiers before being flogged for their blatant disregard of the Voskan officer's authority. Dunia cried out and writhed in agony as she saw her boys dragged before her by the group of men before their commanding officer stepped forth once again in her sitting room.

"As punishment for your disrespect and disobedience, we will be employing both of your sons into national service so that maybe one day they can restore your family name from its tarnished state. As for you madam, who is your Boyar?" the Voskan officer calmly explained, grinning maliciously as his final question left his lips.

"My husband's debt is owed to Boyar Nikolai Surikov, though it is not the business of the Voskan Army." Dunia replied rather coldly.

"Ah yes, but it is the business of a man whose interest is to purchase the property from its owner." his men chuckled behind him as the officer answered with his response. The soldiers held her sons back as Dunia collapsed once again from the devastating shock she'd just received; Petyr and Alexei struggled to rush to their mother's side, but the strength of their multiple oppressors was too strong to break free from their grasp. Besides, both boys were weakened from their beating and they were just as devastated by the news of the whole situation as their mother was. Their father had been taken from them as children and now the army had come to split up what was left of their family; the commanding officer was even going to purchase their mother for use as his own personal whore!

He gave his men the command to take the boys away whilst he undid his pants to test the goods he was contemplating buying. Dunia cried out as her sons screamed for her whilst the heartless soldiers took them away to join the enlisted ranks. That was the last they saw of their mother, though by all accounts the officer had, in fact, bought her from the local Boyar and employed her as one of his many "maids". The officer was no less than a Boyar himself; serving as Captain Ivan Grigorevich Popov in the army, he had used his nobility to secure the rank with ease. In Voska, nobility held significant influence within the military and government when they chose to take an interest in those careers.

Some contented themselves with living their luxurious lives on their lavish estates at the expense of the serfs and peasants that lived on their land. They were given special privilege within the ranks of public office and military, oftentimes being handed the rank at the expense of qualified professionals within the field of a lower social standing. Another example of this was that peasants weren't even allowed to hold any rank above a sergeant in the military and serfs were classed permanently as infantrymen for the entirety of the service, not being considered worthy of a rank or title. So it was that Alexei and Petyr were enlisted as infantrymen with an additional 4 years added to their mandatory 10 year service; they told Petyr that he was being charged as an adult for evading arrest, assisted desertion, and interfering with a legal proceeding, thereby making him eligible to carry out his sentence in national service early.

The brothers were taken away to Giurgiu by means of a military caravan that was comprised of three horse-drawn wagons guided by several squads of Voskan riflemen. The wagons were full of local peasants and townsfolk eligible for enlistment and they were packed into the cramped quarters of the carts like sardines in a tin. The wagons were rather warm and musty from the sweat and condensation that emanated from the caged fodder. From Giurgiu they would travel north via boat up the River Giurgiu to Baia Mara where they would be enlisted into the army and begin their training. It would span the course of two weeks prior to their deployment west into the farthest reaches of Voska's influence in Eastern Aerbon.

CHAPTER FIVE

GREGOV, GORGOVNA

Winter, 2E8

A bullet whizzed off into the night just barely missing Josef's head as he exhaled the lung-full of smoke from his pipe in the dead of the night. Aleksy exclaimed as he ducked for cover alongside his friend and fellow soldier. The pair gripped their muskets tight as they prepared to peek over their cover to check for any signs of movement. A shadowy figure sprinted in the distance racing towards some underbrush twenty meters ahead of him as he attempted to advance on them. Aleksy fired a shot, downing the man as one of his fellows fired on the pair of Voskan sentries, just barely missing them as it shattered the bottle of vodka they kept on a table nearby. Josef swore and returned fire in the direction of the shot whilst Aleksy went about the arduous process of reloading his musket as quickly as he could in the heat of the moment.

"*Privet!*" Aleksy called out in his native tongue at their attackers in an effort to determine their motives.

"*Verpiss dein mutters!*" a Groetshven voice called out in response as he fired upon their position.

"*Blyat*! Is this a declaration of war?" Josef swore as he sought his friend's opinion.

"I don't know... go alert the captain... *Blyat*... What does this mean?" Aleksy fired on the advancing Groetshven forces, though he had no idea how many there were, or anything about them or their motives at all for that matter. Josef ran off into the night to awaken their commanding officer and muster the troops to defend their camp. The military installation in Gregov was rather minimal with roughly 5,000 men to defend it, though each was armed with a standard-issue Voskan musket. The earliest Voskan muskets had been developed in 1E172 and very little had changed about them over the years. Weighing in at 10.5kg, the Voskan musket was significantly heavier than the 9.5kg Groetshven imitation produced in Gewehrstadt, although its Voskan counterpart packed a stronger punch with its .75 calibre shots in comparison to the .69 balls fired by the Groetshven muskets. The result was that Voskan troops were armed with more powerful outdated weaponry whilst the Groetshven troops had the advantage of range and mobility.

This gave the Voskan troops greater damage at the cost of mobility and reloading speed- areas where the Groetshven forces maintained their superiority. This greatly affected the overall tactics of both sides; the Groetshven Confederacy relied greatly on ambushes at long range whilst the Voskan Army would go on to develop a more aggressive mentality, charging their opposition head-on at mid- to close-range whilst seeking cover in their advance to reload at intervals. In the meantime, Aleksy sought to hold off the encroaching enemies whilst awaiting his friend to return with the full force of their company. An alarm went off as watch fires went up, encircling their camp and illuminating the area. Voskan soldiers came stumbling out of the barracks as quickly as they could in the dazed state, quickly scrambling to gather their wits about themselves lest they fall prey to their enemies.

"*Atakovat!* Return fire; we are under attack!" Aleksy called out as his fellow men-in-arms rushed towards him with Josef at their head.

Gunfire erupted from within the camp as they fired upon the retreating Groetshven troops as they made for the treeline of woods that encompassed the camp to the south and the west. More Groetshven marksmen fired upon the Voskan forces in an effort to provide suppressing fire for their retreating countrymen. The majority of those who fell back had fallen to the sharpshooting of their adversaries, though it had done nothing to quell the Groetshven assault. Indeed, the Confederate soldiers assailed them with renewed vigour in an effort to avenge their fallen kinsmen.

"*Ich will dein blut!*" one of the Groetshven infantrymen called out, firing his musket and taking down a nearby soldier. Aleksy saw the head-sized wound in the fallen soldiers chest where he'd fallen just five feet from where Aleksy remained crouched behind the half-wall he took cover behind.

A nearby captain was mustering a squad to charge the enemy forces and push them back, recruiting Aleksy and Josef as soon as he spotted them. Having successfully gathered a group of twelve men, he joined two other squads as they formed a loose company. The leading officer in charge gave the signal and together they ran forth as one unit, picking off their enemies as they spotted them whilst taking cover between shots to reload their muskets. Looking around as he took cover, Aleksy saw that they were not the only company pushing forward; hundreds of Voskan troops charged across the no-man's-land in a desperate effort to drive the Groetshven forces out of Gregov. He loaded another shot into his musket and prepared it before springing out from cover to resume the advance.

CHAPTER SIX

BAIA MARA, VOSKA

Spring, 2E9

Upon completion of their training in Baia Mara, Alexei and Petyr were assigned to two different squads within two separate battalions and they were simultaneously sent to the frontlines of Stangrad and Ivanovo respectively. The Groetshven Confederacy had declared war by laying siege upon the town of Gregov and ransacking it. The Voskan Army had responded by sending troops from Ivanovo, Stangrad, and Kosovo; requesting additional reinforcements to the aforementioned cities to strengthen their defenses should the Groetshven forces prevail. Voska's military officials expected the town of Kosovo to fall to the Groetshven Confederacy and plotted their defense around stalling their advance until the reinforcements from Voska could arrive to drive the Groetshven troops out of Gorgovna once and for all.

"Well, I suppose things could always be worse; at least we're not being sent to Kosovo." Petyr laughed nervously; a fellow soldier standing nearby grunted angrily and walked away with a couple of friends. They were probably being sent to Kosovo themselves, which everyone considered to be a suicide mission.

"Yeah, and besides, we still have some time together before we go our separate ways. It will be fun travelling together seeing more of our homeland." Alexei replied optimistically.

"I'd always wanted to see more of the world; I guess Fate has a strange way of giving us what we ask of it…" Petyr laughed again.

"True, well; I suppose we should get going, the officers are mustering the men it seems." Alexei hoisted his gear and slung it over his shoulders as the rest of his company prepared to depart, falling into formation as the main host gathered together.

Travelling the Iron Highway was a long and arduous ordeal, though it was significantly quicker, easier, and safer than attempting to traverse the rough and jagged Iron Teeth Mountains themselves. Those mountains were so rough and inhospitable that even few amongst the native inhabitants of the region could boast of having travelled further than a couple kilometers from their towns or the highway that connected them. Alexei and Petyr had heard of the Iron Highway, as had the majority of Voska's people, though they had never expected to see it in their lifetimes. The mountains had truly lived up to their expectations; the tall jagged spikes really did look like snow covered teeth with the exposed rocky base looking like the gums that connected all the white fangs that comprised the mountain range. The boys were astounded by the natural beauty of the mountains as their caravan had drawn near, having taken a day's break in Kiev before embarking upon their journey along the Iron Highway.

Taking them up and into the mountains, the highway took them over the Iron River westward towards Gurkā, taking another day's break there as well as the rural mountain towns of Górna and Uzbek as they reached them. Upon breaking fast in the farming town of Uzbek after quartering themselves in the farmsteads of the local inhabitants, the soldiers thanked their hosts and departed immediately onwards towards the land of Gorgovna where they would arrive at the capitol of Istangrad. From there the brothers would part ways as Petyr's company made a southerly trek to Ivanovo whilst Alexei's company marched westward towards the industrial military complex, Stangrad; formerly known during the reign of the Gorgon Empire as Ishtan, a thriving orcish trade city. Another host was sent on a southwesterly course to the town of Kosovo, though their designation was to hold off the Groetshven advance and impede it long enough for more reinforcements to arrive from the mainland.

"Well, I suppose this is where we part ways… I hope one day our family can be reunited." Petyr hugged his brother in the streets of Istangrad as their commanding officers barked orders in preparation for their departure.

"You're going South to Ivanovo; if he survived the attack on Gregov, you will see him there. I hope to see you again one day soon… Goodbye brother." Alexei hesitantly released his brother and waved solemnly as he turned away.

They both knew that they would probably never see each other again and that this was their final farewell; the Voskan Army had torn their entire family apart and scattered them like seeds to be sown in a barren field. The brothers cursed their motherland and damned the army and national service as they marched along, never breaking formation. The brothers went their separate ways and prepared themselves for what would soon come to pass. Confederate troops were already waging their war against the Voskan Army in Kosovo and the city was expected to hold out for no more than a week; Ivanovo and Stangrad were predicted as the two most likely targets to fall under the Groetshven eye in their greedy campaign to take back what they claimed was rightfully theirs.

CHAPTER SEVEN

ROME, ROMAN EMPIRE

Winter, 2E8

"Tobias Schumacher?" a voice inquired after hearing his response to the light knocking at his door.

"*Ja*, what do you want?" he opened the door to find himself face-to-face with a Groetshven officer of the Confederate Army.

"In case you were unaware, the Confederation is in the process of making preparations to declare war upon the Voskan Army and has enacted mandatory national duty for all unemployed or otherwise inactive able-bodied men aged between 16-20 years for a minimum of four years. We were informed by your father that you've abandoned your home to take up life as a vagabond selling your art and discovered that you'd fled here. What you might be unaware of in particular is the fact that under our alliance with Rome I have been granted jurisdiction as an acting officer in the Groetshven Confederate Army to extradite you back to the Confederation for immediate enlistment into national service." the man explained to Tobias in their native tongue.

"*Scheiße…*" Tobias exhaled, feeling the heavy chains of hopelessness take hold over him as he felt his very life-force drain out from his feet, leaving him empty and dumbfounded.

The Groetshven officer put a hand on Tobias' shoulder and calmly asked the lad to gather his things in preparation for their immediate departure. Grabbing the sackcloth bag that contained his clothes and and art supplies, Tobias left behind all of the beautiful portraits of the Roman capitol that he'd painted since his arrival in the city. A carriage awaited them outside the shared house where Tobias took up residence; helping him with his luggage, the officer stowed Tobias' sack in the storage compartment before assisting him aboard the carriage. As soon as the door swung shut behind them the driver pulled out without a moment's notice and before he even knew it Tobias was watching the Roman countryside pass by as the majestic city of Rome shrank away behind them.

"I have to say; you're rather talented as a painter." the officer stirred from where he'd sat in silence across from the young Tobias.

"Thank you sir, but what interest do you have in art? You're a soldier." Tobias replied with genuine surprise and curiosity.

"I was roughly the same age as you when I'd joined the army; my father died a hero in The Gorgon War and I avenged his death, killing those responsible. Before my bloodlust for vengeance took me on the adventure my life led me down as a soldier I too had wanted to see the world. I'm telling you this so that you don't view this time as a time of imprisonment, but rather as an opportunity.

Don't let it break you the way it has those before you." the officer imparted his words of advice upon the young lad as he withdrew a pipe from his coat pocket.

"Who are you?" Tobias inquired.

"My name is Hans, son of Ulrich. I was an infantryman in the Nardic Army during the Gorgon War, but I worked my way up to the rank of an officer over the course of my service." the soldier answered in a rather matter-of-fact tone.

"So you tracked me down all the way to Rome from my father's house?" Tobias replied with yet another question.

"*Nein*; it was more or less random coincidence. I was sent to your family's homestead in search of you and after being informed by your father that you'd run away to take up life as a travelling artist I'd returned to the capitol with the rest of the men I'd mustered. The Kaiser sent me personally on an errand here in Rome where I heard tales of a Groetshven painter who busked in the streets of the city-centre, so I did a little investigating before deciding to pay you a visit. I hope you don't mind that I decided to keep one of the paintings you left behind for myself by the way…" the officer replied, extracting the canvas in question to reveal to it's creator. The painting was a portrait of Baiern's port in Dusseldorf; ironically enough the shared hometown of both Hans and Tobias prior to the Nardic invasion of Gilan, rewritten in the Confederation of Groetshven's history regarding the events of the Gorgon War.

"So what opportunity have you found during your time serving the Confederacy?" Tobias inquired hesitantly after a brief moment of thoughtful silence.

"I beg your pardon?" the officer seemed momentarily confused, as if the question had appeared out of thin air.

"You told me not to view my service as a punishment, but rather an opportunity. What did the army give you?" Tobias replied.

"It gave me catharsis; a way to deal with the loss of my family; I haven't seen any of them since the War. It taught me many valuable life lessons, but most importantly it gave me a sense of fulfillment." Hans looked back on his life, thoughtfully reflecting on the time he'd spent as a soldier before answering the lad's question.

"I don't mean to be rude sir, but it would seem rather that the military tore your family apart and that you found the means to accept it within yourself." Tobias replied rather smartly.

"Ah, but isn't that life? We're thrown into a situation that by all rights should break us down and yet we manage to find a way to overcome it and accept the reality of it for what it was. Do you think of yourself to be special? Individually hand-selected by some great deity and given your own voice to say, "stop, you can't do this to me; it isn't fair!" Unfortunately this is the world we live in and there are no magical deities; the Old Gods are dead. Just as we were thust into our lives without a choice, so too is everyone else you will ever meet and all we have that separates us is our decisions. One day you'll understand this fact of life too, and maybe then you will accept it." Hans gave his response to the young lad's smug demeanor.

"I see now why you picked our hometown." Tobias retorted as he turned his attention by to the window as the scenery passed them by.

"*Wie bitte**?" Hans inquired, once again befuddled by the rather unusual youth.

*Sorry. Used in the same context as "excuse me" or "come again?"

"It makes sense that you would take our hometown out of the whole lot of paintings, since that's the only place you'll probably never see again." Tobias replied rather dreamily as he gazed out the window.

"Yes, you're probably right…" Han's voice trailed off as he contented himself to stare out of his own passenger window and the pair sat in silence together for the remainder of the trip.

CHAPTER EIGHT

GREGOV, GORGOVNA

Winter, 2E8

During his training in Gewehrstadt, Tobias didn't even bother to visit his family. He was sure his father had given his information to the Confederation's men out of spite in order to teach his son one of life's harsher messages and for that Tobias could never forgive him. The lad received some brief training in close quarters combat with knives and a sword, though it was predominantly focused on long-range marksmanship with muskets, following drills, and practising a handful of formations. He spent most of his free-time in the town's military barracks, though he'd made a couple of friends that inevitably ended up inviting him out for drinks at one of the local pubs. Tobias and the lads became friends over the course of their training and before they knew it, Erik, Steffan, and Marc found themselves being shoved aboard the caravans one by one alongside their new friend, boarding the wagon that would deliver them to the battlefield far away in the Voskan lands of Gorgovna.

The wagon ride had been peaceful, as had the night's rest they'd received upon their arrival at the Groetshven camp situated 7km southwest of the Voskan town of Gregov. Following their uneventful sleep, the soldiers were awakened to the news that they would be deploying to assail Gregov at midnight. Tobias and his newfound friends were anxious of the upcoming battle; Erik had come from a background of military service and so he was somewhat eager to prove himself and join his ancestors as a battle-hardened veteran of war whilst Marc and Steffan were nervous of what to expect. Steffan, like Tobias and Erik, had also come from a family of soldiers, though he had been content with his life on his father's farmstead and had little interest in the art of war and killing. Marc, on the other hand, was a bit older than the other lads being twenty years of age himself, and he was freshly unemployed after being fired from Gewehrstadt's arms factory for sleeping on the job.

"*Scheiße*; why don't we just wake a whole army of bears at night and set ourselves ablaze?" Marc muttered as the boys gathered their gear in preparation for their deployment.

"*Niemand kann seinem Tött entkommen**!" Erik laughed as he grabbed his personal supply of ammunition for the musket he carried slung over his shoulder.

"*Wie bitte?* Is that meant to be positive, or are you advising us to accept the inevitable?" Steffan replied, rather perturbed by Erik's excitement.

"Both! And why not? At least we can take as many of their souls with us before we return to the Void." Erik answered without a moment's hesitation.

*No man can escape his death.

So it was that the lads made their final preparations and spent their final day before the battle drinking, laughing, joking, and smoking between themselves as if they'd known each other for years rather than just the last of couple weeks. The time quickly passed them by and before they knew it the lads were being herded back into the wagons where they would be driven away to the outskirts of the city to make their declaration of war in what they were unanimously calling a *blitzkrieg*. No one spoke aboard the wagons as every man aboard prepared himself for the assault. None knew what to expect and so they mentally prepared themselves to accept their fates whatever they may be. Tobias drew in a small sketchbook he carried with him, drawing his immediate surroundings within the wagon as the caravans drove along.

"*Das ist gut*! You should draw one of me next so I can send it home to *mein mutter*!" Steffan spoke up.

"*Ja*! Of course; I can do one for each of you!" Tobias grinned, happy to draw the portraits of his new friends after seeing their interest in his deepest passion.

Over the course of the journey he drew each of them; shortly after finishing the final portrait of Marc, the wagons came to a stop and the officers barked the command to disembark. They were surrounded by light woods and small shrubbery all around, though as their officers guided them along the Groetshven troops started to see the trees thin out until before long they were staring upon the town of Gregov. They could see the shadowy outline of the town in the distance as the woods ended and gave way to flat rolling plains. They encroached themselves upon the town at the woods' edge, lining up along the treeline, awaiting the command to attack. Each soldier drew his musket to eye level and crouched down in preparation. One squad was given the order to move in, scouting out the town and initiating the attack. Eight other companies circled around the town's outskirts to provide multiple angles of covering and suppressing fire when the time came.

A little red pinprick of light went up in the distance as a Voskan sentry puffed on his pipe. A gunshot cracked off, shattering the silence of the night that hung over them and initiating the assault of the small Voskan border town. The Voskan sentry returned fire, assisted by one other. Several Groetshven troops fell to the pair of Voskan watchmen as they returned fire in an attempt to ward off their attackers. The Groetshven officers ordered their men to fire in small groups to divert the enemy's attention so that they could redirect the majority of the Confederate forces to the northeastern end of the town and essentially flank the Voskan troops from behind.

"*Atakovat!*" A Voskan officer could be heard faintly as an alarm went up in the enemy camp.

"*Feuer frei!*" a captain issued the order to attack and immediately the Groetshven troops rained down suppressing fire on the Voskan forces.

The Groetshven troops charged forward, firing upon the Voskan forces in waves as they reloaded their muskets on the run. Returning fire, the Voskan troops took turns between firing and ducking behind whatever cover they could find to take refuge behind whilst they Groetshven forces swarmed the town by force from the south to provide a distraction for the greater host that would flank their enemies from behind. Tobias dropped down to the ground as a bullet flew past him and another embedded itself in Marc's chest just ahead of him, downing the lad as Tobias laid gripping his musket just feet away. *Scheiße, that could have been me*, Tobias thought to himself initially before coming to the realisation that his friend had just been shot just in front of him, staring with horror as he gurgled blood from the sides of his mouth, reaching out to Tobias in total agony as he desperately sought help of some sort.

"*Bitte*,* kill me…" Marc gasped as he attempted to crawl towards Tobias on his belly, wincing in pain as the desperation burned in his eyes.

"*Nein*! No, I can't!" Tobias squirmed away as he pushed himself up upon his feet to resume charging the enemy forces, running from the thought of his dying friend as he tried to wipe it from his mind.

*Groetshven, translates to "please"

Bullets flew in every direction as the Groetshven forces assailed the Voskan outpost, though soon the enemy forces rushed out to greet them, driving their Groetshven attackers back towards the treeline from whence they came. Even as the Confederate troops fell back, the greater part of their host came swooping in from the north, slaughtering the unsuspecting enemies from behind as all their attention remained focused on their southern assailants. It was a total bloodbath as nearly 12,000 Groetshven troops descended upon the town of less than 5,000. Voskan inhabitants. Tobias rushed after Erik and Steffan as they rushed towards the outskirts of the small town whilst dodging gunfire. Taking cover behind the wall of a small cottage, Tobias peeked around the corner and fired off a shot at one of the Voskan soldiers firing on his fellow countrymen as his friends simultaneously took down two of the soldier's squad-mates.

"*Geil*! Nice shooting!" Steffan called out with glee.

"*Dein blut riechst so gut**!" Erik called out, taunting the Voskan troops in their native language.

"*Du bist irre*[‡]!" Tobias exclaimed as they reloaded their muskets whilst the four remaining soldiers that comprised the enemy platoon rushed for cover, returning fire upon the Groetshven lads as they ran.

* Your blood smells (so/very) good!

[‡] You're crazy!

A handful of fellow reinforcements came to the aid of Tobias and his friends and together they eliminated the remnants of the enemy Voskan squad. The grateful lads thanked their fellow countrymen before continuing their unified advance into the heart of the town. They would push the Voskan defenders back, into the hungry jowls of the greater Groetshven host that assailed the town from the North. Their sole goal was to survive whilst the Voskan troops predominantly focused on the initial southern assault, not realising that it was no more than a diversion to provide the northern forces with enough time to position their troops throughout the town. Once the numerous companies comprising the main Confederate host were positioned at their vantage points, the musketeers rained fire from above down upon their enemies whilst the southern companies continued to provide suppressing and covering fire.

CHAPTER NINE

IVANOVO, GORGOVNA

Summer, 2E9

Petyr reloaded his musket and fired on the advancing Groetshven troops. The Confederate soldiers took advantage of the cover that the Gregovian Forest provided them whilst heavy gunfire resounded all around from both sides as the hostile forces fired upon one another in turns. Petyr aimed down the sights of his short-barrel musket and fired on a long-range musketeer even as the man picked off one of his kinsmen. Upon killing the enemy soldier, he broke free from the cover of the hay bale he hid behind and sprinted ahead towards another bale even as the Groetshven troops fired upon the Voskan town and its defenders. He fired off another shot into the treeline alongside several of his fellow kinsmen as they provided suppressing fire to cover the advance of the Voskan host. All around the Voskan forces were racing forth as they fanned out, covering as much land and making themselves as small a target as they could in order to hunt down and thwart the Confederate troops.

"*Nastupleniye*! *Atakovat zelyonka*!*" an officer called out, ordering his men to advance and direct their attack upon the woods their enemy used for cover.

*Voskan translation; "Advance! Attack the woods**"

**Zelyonka was a slang term used by the Voskan Army for woods or vegetation that could be used to take cover behind, the actual translation being "brilliant green medicine"

Petyr continued to advance in formation with the loose company he served under, picking off the Groetshven snipers one by one with the help of his squad-mates as they kept low running in and out of whatever cover they could find. A cry went up as *Blitztruppen* managed to flank Ivanovo from both the North and the East ends of town, slaughtering the sentries and troops occupying the area with a few volleys of gunfire. Petyr dropped down on his belly and laid silently in the grassy field whilst the war raged on around him. He slowly crawled across the no-man's-land on a westerly course in an attempt to break through the Groetshven frontlines and put as much distance between himself and the war as he could. Upon breaking through the Groetshven frontlines of the assault on Ivanovo, Petyr leapt to his feet and put all of his energy into the sprint as he ran for his life. The sounds of gunfire began to die down an faded away as Petyr ventured further and further from the battlefield.

Day gave way to night and before he knew it Petyr was watching the sun rise on the second day of his journey. He had no idea where he was going and the Voskan youth hardly had any rations or ammunition; Petyr was stranded and left for dead in a place he'd only heard tales of. Left without any other options besides continuing onward, he aimlessly stumbled along through the wilderness of Gorgovna in search of something. Anything was better than sitting around waiting for death to find him, though he was steadily losing faith with every passing hour. Before long he'd ended up using all of his food and water on the three day trek, though he was seemingly no closer to anywhere than when he'd first begun the arduous journey. Surrounding the Voskan youth in every direction, the flat grassy plain were dotted with trees and vegetation, though the scenery hadn't changed whatsoever throughout the entirety of his desperate venture.

For all he knew, the lad could have been walking around in circles the whole time and he'd be none the wiser. The sky was always overcast in those lands and so the sun dimly shone through the cloud cover, though it always appeared as a blurry golden patch behind the grey curtain that hung over Gorgovna and the northernmost reaches of the Groetshven Confederation. Several more days passed by and the Voskan deserter lost count after some time. With his rations depleted, Petyr cried out to the dreary grey heavens as he sank to his knees in defeat. He'd finally given up. *After all; what does it matter anyways?* Petyr asked himself. If he went back to Voska he'd be tried and executed for desertion, if the Confederates captured him he'd be a prisoner of war, and if he continued on in his attempt to survive he'd die alone after countless days of suffering in the wilderness. *No, it's better this way*, he thought to himself as he curled up into the foetal position.

Petyr had no way of knowing how long he'd been lying on the ground, though after some time he heard the sounds of an approaching convoy. The distant sound of horses, wagons, and men steadily grew in volume until finally they were upon him and still he laid there on the ground; too overwhelmed by his own emotions to move. Hoping that they would just trample him, the young lad wished for a quick and easy death, though he would soon find out that it was not in his destiny to die such a death. He could hear voices as the soldiers drew near and by their accents and the language they spoke, he was able to deduce that they were Confederates. *Blyat, just kill me already*, Petyr thought to himself as he attempted to drift off into sleep. Suddenly he felt a pair of hands roll him over and lift him by his armpits as a Groetshven soldier dragged him to his feet before shaking him.

"*Wach auf! Wach auf!*" the man shook Petyr awake, though the boy appeared no livelier with his eyes open than closed.

"*Setzen sie ihn an seinen platz.*" a Groetshven officer called out as he approached the pair, ordering his inferior to put their newfound prisoner with the rest.

So it was that the Confederate soldiers loaded him aboard one of the wagons they set aside for the transportation of prisoners. Petyr could see the judgement in their eyes as the Confederates passed him by without breaking pace in their forward march. The soldier that carried him slung over the shoulder like a sack of potatoes dropped him down on the floor of the prison wagon before returning to formation. Looking around, Petyr stared upon the cold, hardened, and weary faces of his fellow captured countrymen. The Voskan prisoners glared at him in silence, staring him down as if he were some sort of wretched abomination.

"*Privet?*" Petyr spoke up sheepishly as he cast his eyes down to avoid their cold gaze.

"Do not speak with us, *izmennik.**" one of them replied.

*Voskan derogatory term, equivalent of "traitor/backstabber"

"*Idi nakhuy neudachnik*!*" Petyr exclaimed, "I see you didn't give your lives for the motherland either."

"*Blyat cyka*; you have a lot of fight in you for an *izmennik*." another prisoner spoke up in response, spitting in Petyr's face.

"Was it the lack of fight in you that brought you here?" Petyr shot back with a malicious grin as he wiped the spit off his face.

*Voskan; "Go fuck yourself loser"

CHAPTER TEN

KOSOVO, GORGOVNA

Spring, 2E9

"Tobias, they're ordering us to prepare for departure!" Steffan called out to his friend hurriedly. The young painter had seated himself in the heart of the city centre where the Confederate soldiers had piled up the corpses of their Voskan enemies to rot.

"I'm almost finished…" Tobias muttered as he finished up his gruesome portrait of the traumatic scene.

"*Sich beeilen*!* They're about to leave!" Steffan grasped his friend by the shoulder, staring into the young painter's traumatised eyes.

"I'm almost done; I want to capture this moment while it's still fresh." Tobias murmured, listlessly gazing past Steffan into the distance.

*Groetshven translation; "Hurry up."

"*Nein*; there is no time for that! We must depart now!" Steffan grabbed the lad and dragged him away. Tobias clung to his art and supplies as Steffan took him along, racing to fall into rank and formation as the host disembarked from the city.

Leaving the city, the Confederate host set their sights on Ivanovo whilst a secondary force was already en route to the installation that was Voska's military stronghold, Stangrad. Ivanovo was a town comprised of warehouses and a small military compound where their Aerbon-based musket-manufacturing facility was situated. It was in Groetshven's greater interest to seize the city intact whilst the Voskan forces had been ordered to defend it until the last man; told to raze themselves along with the town should they fail in the endeavour. In Stangrad the Groetshven forces were armed with cannon and artillery so that they could lay siege upon the mighty fortress and decimate their opposition in the process. From there, the two separate Confederate hosts would unite to drive the Voskan Army out of Gorgovna once and for all by seizing the capitol of Istangrad.

If the Confederation of Groetshven could take Istangrad it would effectively cut off Voska's access to Gorgovna via the Iron Highway, leaving their colonies in the barren Northern Wastes to disintegrate in the ensuing instability. Meanwhile, the Confederation would make moves to strengthen their hold over the former Voskan State of Gorgovna and rebuild the war-torn cities before populating them with the farmers and peasants that were the backbone of their production and economy. So it was that Tobias and his friends travelled in formation with the Groetshven host on their journey to Ivanovo. Tobias had become somewhat more reclusive following the recent events of the Confederacy's past two battles. Seeing the countless deaths of his fellow countrymen as well as his friend had had a massive impact on the young painter and he expressed it vividly and realistically through his art. The drawing book he'd taken with him everywhere since he'd bought it in Rome had transitioned from portraits of the Roman, Groetshven, and Gorgovnian scenery and towns to portraits of his friends to the dying face of Marc, corpses piled in the fields, war-devastated towns and ruinous buildings, and death in general.

"*Wei gehts*? You've seemed more distant of late; are you alright?" Steffan spoke up as they marched along.

"*Ja*, where is your national pride? We're driving the enemy out of our rightful lands! You should be grateful to be apart of such a vital part of the Confederation's history!" Erik exclaimed, rather irritated by the recent mood and behaviour of his friend.

Rather than respond to the concern of his friends, Tobias continued to march in formation without speaking; the light that had once shined bright in his eyes had dimmed and his gaze remained fixedly downcast and distant.

'What's so important about these pictures you care about so much anyways?" Erik said as he snatched the notebook from Tobias' satchel to skim through its contents.

"*Scheiße...*" the proud youth murmured after a moment as the art transitioned from beautiful landscapes to the traumatic horrors of death and warfare. Erik stared upon the countless dead faces, bodies piled in streets, the ruinous remains of Voskan towns, and the pleading look on their dying friend's face as he reached out for help in his final moments. It shattered his mind and broke his soul; Steffan exhaled deeply and fell out of formation as he stopped dead in his tracks where he'd been peering over Erik's shoulder to catch a glimpse himself. The line behind of men behind them continued ceaselessly, jolting Steffan out of his shock as they shoved him forward. Taking the notebook back from Erik, Tobias continued onwards in silence as his friends joined him in his dissociated state. Together they followed their fellow countrymen on the northern trek to Ivanovo and they spoke no more.

CHAPTER ELEVEN

STANGRAD, GORGOVNA

Summer, 2E9

The ground shook as Groetshven catapults flung their boulders over the mighty walls of Stangrad where they came crashing down upon the buildings that troops that comprised Voska's seemingly impenetrable fortress. Alexei and his fellow countrymen scattered in all directions as they sought to evade the devastatingly deadly chunks of rock as buildings collapsed and boulders rained down from above. Utilising the cannons, ballistae, and trebuchets that lined the parapets surrounding the city, the Voskan forces stood their ground in an attempt to ward off the Confederation's initial assault. It was a futile effort; the Groetshven siege machines fired upon the Voskan stronghold relentlessly and its walls began to yield to the might of the Confederate artillery. Voskan troops could even be seen leaping to their deaths as the colossal boulders came hurtling towards their positions where they manned the turrets in an attempt to ward off the Groetshven advance.

"*Blyat*! It is hopeless; we're all going to die here!" a nearby soldier called out in his desperation to escape.

"Spoken like a true *izmennik*; I'm sure your family is proud." his captain rebutted as he mustered Alexei and the rest of his company to prepare for a counter-attack.

"If there are any of you here that still have even a shred of honour left; join me now and you may yet survive. As for the rest of you; feel free to join the *izmennik* and run as far from here as you can before I change my mind and have you executed as the traitors that you are… Hurry; the Confederates won't be so kind if they catch you." the captain spoke, banishing the deserters with a wave of his hand.

"But *kapitan*…" the soldier stammered pleadingly in an attempt to take back his previous words.

"*Zatknis izmennik!*" the commander turned on his heel and casually lopped the man's head off with a single swing of his ceremonial blade. Although Voskan officers' swords were predominantly decorative, every blade was sharpened so that in the event it was used the sword could still serve it's original purpose.

Staring into the hardened faces of those who stood before him, the captain waited to see if anyone else would follow in the footsteps of their fallen comrade-in-arms and desert. No one moved an inch. After a moment he congratulated them and laughed, telling them that if any one of them had decided to turn and flee he would have ordered their remaining countrymen to turn and fire upon them. Alexei breathed a sigh of relief, having realised that he had, in fact, made the right decision by standing his ground. The lad had pondered for a moment whether he should turn and flee or stand and fight, so the captain's cruel words resonated within him.

That could have been me, he thought as he stared upon the dead man's headless corpse, thanking fate that the man's face was turned away to prevent him from catching the listless gaze of death. Alexei attempted to shake the feeling of unease as his mind snapped back to the present just in time to hear the conclusion of his commander's brief speech, ordering the men to execute the orders he just finished giving them. With no idea what was going on, Alexei formed up with his fellow squad-mates and followed them as the soldiers sprinted towards Stangrad's northern entrance. The sounds of gunfire and crashing booms from cannons, catapults, and trebuchets grew fainter as they drew closer to the North Gate until finally the Voskan troops felt some relief from the sense of impending doom that beset them. Their commander barked an order at one of the men guarding the gate, though his authority was immediately challenged.

"Open the gates; we're attacking from the rear!" he called out to the gate keepers.

"*Da neuzheli? Ty mozhesh'v eto poverit**?!?" one of the gate keepers exclaimed to his companion.

*Voskan translation; "Oh really? Can you believe it?"

"*Blyat; posmotri na etogo cyka predatelya*!*" his friend replied with a chuckle as they aimed their muskets at the captain without a moment's hesitation.

"*Idi nakhuy*! I am *Polkovodets* of these men and I demand passage! Who dares deny me?!" the captain snapped harshly, though neither of the watchmen lowered their muskets.

"*Cyka blyat*; you're no *polkovodets*, more like a *pekhotinets*." the first guard replied with a laugh.**

"*Atakovat*!" the captain barked his order whilst simultaneously jumping out of the way as the pair of gate keepers fired upon him and his men. Dazed and confused, Alexei joined his fellow countrymen as they unleashed a volley of gunfire upon their own friendly forces, killing the pair of watchmen under the strict orders of their own captain. He ordered them to open the gate even as more reinforcements arrived to join them in the counter-strike. They poured out of the city in what was meant to be an attempt to flank the Groetshven forces, though they hadn't planned on the Confederate forces flanking them…

*Voskan translation; "Fuck; listen to this bitch traitor!"

*A *polkovodets* is a commanding officer, whereas a *pekhotinets* is no more than a basic infantryman.

Alexei and his fellow kinsmen found that they had accidentally stumbled upon an ambush. The Groetshven forces had been diverting their enemy's attention towards the southern assault whilst a secondary host comprised entirely of infantry soldiers and marksmen had been making their way around to infiltrate and flank the Voskan stronghold from behind; this plan had worked in their previous battles and so it remained the primary tactic of the Confederation's *blitzkrieg* attacks. This time however, things had gone awry when the Voskan troops sought to use the element of surprise to flank their enemies from an unexpected direction as well.

CHAPTER TWELVE

IVANOVO, GORGOVNA

Summer, 2E9

"*Cyka blyat*!" a Voskan soldier call out as he cracked off a shot in the direction of where Tobias hid behind a handful of crates and barrels. Jumping out from behind the cover, Tobias returned fire, hitting the man in his hip and watching as he crumpled to the ground in agonising pain. Ducking back into the cover, the Groetshven artist-turned-soldier reloaded his musket as his compatriots ran ahead a ways in the forward assault. Steffan fired a round nearby before charging towards a small cottage to take cover behind on of it's walls, but took a bullet in the process of advancing. The lead ball shattered his arm, knocking him off his feet as he let loose a shriek of pain.

"*Scheiβe*; stay down!" Erik called out from not far away, seeing his injured friend attempt to push himself back up to his feet. Bullets whizzed in every direction and men fell on both sides.

"*Bedecke mich*!*" Tobias shouted as he raced out from his own cover to rescue his fallen friend.

*Groetshven translation; "cover me"

Rushing towards Steffan where he laid writhing on the ground in agony, Tobias ducked under the gunfire whilst his fellow countrymen provided suppressing fire, taking down a handful of their enemies in the process. A lead ball ricocheted off the wall and just barely missed his head as Tobias reached his friend, taking a knee as he returned fire upon the soldier that had tried to shoot him. He pulled the trigger and sent a shot flying into the chest of his attacker; watching as the bullet embedded itself in the Voskan soldier, shattering his rib cage. Steffan continued to moan as he keeled over in agonising pain; Tobias lifted the wounded lad to his feet and together they stumbled towards the cover of the cottage.

"*Verpiss mich*; you saved me… *Du*… You should have left me alone…" Steffan struggled to speak from the severity of his pain.

"Look at you! They only got your arm; you can still make it yet!" Tobias replied, attempting to talk his friend out of the hopelessness he was drowning in.

"I can't fight like this… They're going to take my arm… You've damned me to a life as a cripple…" Steffan griped.

"So they'll probably send you home; you've served your time! I wish it could be me in your place!" Tobias shot back, viewing his friend as ungrateful.

"I wish it had been you... Maybe then you'd see my pain, painter. What will my family think of me? That I wasn't even good enough to die for my home?" Steffan used his good arm to prop himself against the wall as he lit himself a pipe of tobacco, coughing as he did so.

Another bullet ricocheted off the corner of the wall they hid behind, reminding Tobias of their surroundings. His mind returned to the heat of the moment and so he popped out from behind the cottage to fire upon another Voskan soldier before returning to his previous position to reload. He told Steffan to hang back and keep quiet whilst he continued to fight off their attackers. Erik rushed towards them with a couple fellow soldiers and together the group gathered around whilst the fighting continued in an effort to find a way to evacuate the injured lad. They took turns shooting and reloading whilst Tobias and Erik attempted to lift Steffan to his feet, guiding the lightheaded youth along even as the blood-loss began to affect him.

"*Die ende ist nahe...*" Steffan groaned, feeling his consciousness fading as they hurriedly dragged him along.

"*Sich beeilen!*" Tobias joked with Steffan, "*Kämpfen bis zum schluss!*"

"There you go, finally some fire in you!" Erik exclaimed in response to Tobias, repeating him as he shouted for all to hear; "Fight until the end!"

CHAPTER THIRTEEN

STANGRAD, GORGOVNA

Summer, 2E9

"*Atakovat*; fight for your worthless lives!" Alexei's commander called out, brandishing his sword as he led the charge.

Not having expected any resistance or the northern end of the city, the Groetshven troops broke rank and fell back. The initial volley of Voskan gunfire took down several Confederate saboteurs whilst the survivors sought whatever cover they could find, though there was significantly less vegetation in the northern reaches of Gorgovna compared to the South. Those who managed to find cover returned fire upon Stangrad's defenders in an effort to provide suppressing fire for their fellow countrymen to give them more time to make their retreat. The Groetshven company continued to pick off as many Voskan soldiers they could, though they were significantly outnumbered; the main purpose of their plan was to utilise the explosives they carried with them to breach the North Gate and stealthily grant the southern host entry into the city by opening the gates from within.

With the plan having fallen apart, the Confederate forces attempted to split their company into two groups, one covering the other so that they could fall back and regroup whilst the Voskan troops charged forth and assailed them. Alexei and his comrades burst forth like a pack of wolves charging after their prey, pushing the Groetshven company south and west back the way they'd come. Meanwhile in the southern portion of the city their militaristic strength was proving insufficient to hold off the Groetshven host any longer. The siege weapons of the Groetshven host had devastated the fortress' walls and the main gate was giving way to their battering rams as they waged their assault. A handful of saboteurs had even managed to make their way towards the West Gate where they busied themselves with planting the explosives before any of Alexei's compatriots could stop them whilst more of the Confederacy's southern forces made their way North to join them in their attempt to breach the western district of Stangrad's outer wall.

"*Blyat*! It's no use; they're taking the city!" one of the soldiers called out as an explosive blast signaled that the Confederate forces had managed to breach the wall. Smoke poured from the city as catapulted boulders continued to rain down whilst the buildings fell before their might. Stangrad was steadily being reduced to rubble and still the Voskan troops ceaselessly continued in their futile efforts to defend the stronghold.

"*Deine kämpfe sind meine freude!*" one of the Groetshven soldiers shouted, taunting the Voskan forces in his native tongue.

"*Idi nakhuy cyka!*" Alexei shouted back, picking out the man that challenged his nation and shooting him down.

"Who is the brave man that thinks he can challenge the might of Voska comrade?" one of Alexei's squad-mates called out jokingly after witnessing the well-placed shot to the Confederate soldier's stomach. It would be a slow and agonising death for the cocky grunt as he slowly bled out over the course of several hours. *Maybe that will teach you the price of arrogance*, Alexei thought to himself, relishing in the bittersweet satisfaction of the life he'd taken.

"Verpiss du und deine mutters!" a Groetshven soldier replied as he and his squad fired upon Alexei's position. The Voskan troops ducked into cover before returning fire, catching a few of the Confederates that had been slow taking cover themselves. Both sides took a moment to reload whilst Groetshven reinforcements arrived to let loose another volley in an effort to cover the advance of their kinsmen.

"Stand your ground; to the last man!" one of the Voskan officers called out as they continued to fend of the advancing Confederate forces. It was no use. The Groetshven troops were already overrunning the city and the majority of the Voskan forces had either been killed or captured. Alexei and the remnants of the Voskan Army stationed in Stangrad were steadily being picked off one by one as the Confederate soldiers focused their undivided attention on the survivors of their *blitzkrieg*.

"*Yebat' eto*; for what purpose should we die!?" one of the Voskan troops called out. He fired alongside his squad and called out for a retreat. The officers demanded their companies stand their ground, but it was too late- the retreat was in motion. Alexei fell back alongside his squad, ignoring as their captain called after them. They turned and let loose some suppressing fire alongside several other squads in their company to cover the rest of the remnant battalion's retreat. The officers saw the futility in remaining behind as the Groetshven forces continued to advance and fire upon them in an effort to capture them as prisoners of war. So it was that the city of Stangrad fell to the Groetshven Confederation and the remaining Voskan troops retreated North in a last-ditch effort to escape the invading conquerors.

CHAPTER FOURTEEN

STANGRAD, GORGOVNA

Summer, 2E9

The ground shook as Groetshven siege engines rolled along on their path to Stangrad's heavily fortified southern entrance whilst the city's mighty walls trembled from the terrible force of the boulders flung by .Confederate catapults in devastating volleys. Tobias and his squad continued on their own course separate from the main host. Their objective was to breach the Voskan fortress from the West using experimental explosives whilst another breakaway battalion did the same from the North. Keeping close to the vegetation and sparse cover of trees that dotted the land so close to the banks of Lake Ishtan, Nils Hönig and his brothers in arms trekked along as stealthily as they could on their trek towards the western entrance into Stangrad.

Once they were in position, the captains ordered their men to wait so that the squads that continued onwards had time to reach their own objective; the North Gate. If the plan was to succeed their attacks had to be coordinated simultaneously and so they waited on their brethren, taking advantage of the moment to prepare themselves for what was soon to come to pass. Gripping his musket tight, the corporal turned to one of his squad-mates- no more than a lowly musketeer the same as he had been before his promotion- to ask the lad if he was alright. Laughing, the young and inexperienced infantryman chuckled and asked "under what circumstances?" with a slight grin on his face. The pair exchanged the smirk before Nils wished his fellow luck in the impending firefight they'd be running into. The boy laughed and replied that he didn't need gods or luck; he came from a bloodline of soldiers.

"The only thing a surname is good for is inheriting a title." Nils chuckled.

"It will take more than a piece of metal to kill Helmut Nitzsch…" the lad replied solemnly, simultaneously introducing himself.

"That's probably a popular quote amongst the countless soldiers before you and I'm sure you won't be the last to say it." Nils answered, humbled by the thought.

"And I can guarantee that this won't be the last time I'm heard saying it either." Helmut joked, unafraid of the future and what it held.

"Nothing is life is guaranteed, except for death and the sun's daily rise and fall." Nils concluded, staring into the depths of the young lad's eyes and into his very soul. The boy seemed rather nervous, though he was rather cocky and arrogant in his outward appearance.

"*Ja*, that may be true, but I'm still here at the end of it all." Helmut replied.

"At the end of it all? The real war hasn't even begun yet." Nils said, abruptly ending the conversation, no longer desiring to indulge in his newfound friend's thoughts.

"Perhaps you're right." the youth conceded, falling into silence as he waited with his friend for the order to attack.

Finally their officers ordered the squads to deploy and advance upon the Voskan fortress' entrance and so they departed from where they took cover to span the land between themselves and their objective. With their attention focused on the southern assault, the Voskan forces were totally unprepared for the western and northern saboteurs that charged forth with full speed. Helmut and Nils' squad slowed down halfway between their starting point and the West Gate alongside their squad to provide suppressing fire and support should they be detected. The first squad reached their objective whilst the engineers began setting up the explosives. Gunfire erupted from the North and Nils' company readied themselves in preparation, should the Voskan troops become aware of their presence.

Groetshven troops could be seen in the distance falling back as a host of Voskan troops pushed them back. The engineers rushed to conclude their task as quickly as they could before the northern defenders of the fortress overtook them. The northern forces approached and called out to the fellow countrymen in a request for support as the Voskan troops continued to pick them off and push them back. Nils, Helmut, and their brothers in arms offered what little support they could, returning fire on their attackers in an effort to cover the retreat as the engineers finished up with their task. Bullets whizzed by as the Voskan soldiers continued their advance, undeterred by the gunfire of their enemies.

"We did it, we did it; it's done!" one of the engineers cried out gleefully as they turned and sprinted with all their might from the western entrance.

"*Verpiss du,* Voskan *müll!*" Helmut laughed, taunting their attackers as he turned and fell back alongside Nils.

"*Scheiße!*" Nils exclaimed as the explosives detonated, blasting the West Gate to smithereens, along with several of the Voskan forces that pursued them. The Groetshven troops fell back towards the North Gate even as it fell before the might of the greater Groetshven host. From there they would invade the fort and slaughter it's occupants in their conquest, claiming the remains of the mighty stronghold in the name of the Groetshven Confederation. Spotting the northern retreat, a handful of companies comprising the greater southern host broke off to come to the aid of their fellows as the Voskan forces continued to push them back.

"*Ich will dein blut; dein angst riechst so gut!*" Helmut called out gleefully as he turned to taunt and fire upon the Voskan forces. Nils joined him as they covered the retreat whilst the Voskan soldiers returned fire upon them, taking down some of their kinsmen.

"*Ich bin verlorn*; I can't see!" a Confederate soldier called out grasping around blindly as he ran with a hand covering his eyes, bleeding from the musket shot that grazed his face across his eyes, tearing a chunk of flesh from the bridge of his nose.

The Groetshven soldiers stood their ground and fended off their northern attackers, forcing the inferior forces to fall back and retreat whilst the main host of the Confederation took the city by force, killing all of its inhabitants. Whilst their kinsmen hunted down the remnants of the retreating Voskan troops outside the walled stronghold Nils and Helmut entered the city, joining their squad as the main host rounded up the remaining Voskan soldiers to capture and send away to Nuremberg to work in the prison camp. There they would be kept locked away in the cramped prison cells when they weren't busy labouring in the mines or the lumber yard under constant watch. Helping their fellows oversee the whole affair, Nils took a moment to pack some Nardic tobacco into his pipe whilst Helmut relished in witnessing the proud Voskan soldiers humbled by their defeat as they were rounded up loaded aboard the prison wagons like livestock. Following their victory, the Groetshven troops sent the wagons away to Nuremberg Prison with the rest of the Voskan prisoners of war whilst they themselves prepared to depart from their place to Istangrad. There though would provide artillery and infantry support for the Confederate forces already en route to the capitol on their way from Ivanovo.

CHAPTER FIFTEEN

IVANOVO, GORGOVNA

Summer, 2E9

"Goodbye my friends... Thank you Tobias... If it wasn't for you I'd be dead." Steffan reached out to hold his friends' hands one last time before the caravan he'd been put into departed from that place. He was being sent back home to his family's home where they would take care of him on his road to recovery. The medics had amputated his wounded arm and marked him unfit for service, returning him to his father's farm in Hamburg, though he'd be bedridden for some time as the doctors had informed him. They'd suggested that he spend the majority of his time getting as much rest as he could lest the injury become infected. Tobias and Erik bid their farewells; their hearts were heavy at the loss of yet another friend, but they rejoiced that he was not dead and at the fact that he was free from the devastating trauma of war they'd come to get used to during their enlistment.

"I did what any of us would have done; you don't have to thank me..." Tobias' voice trailed off.

"*Ja*; we're brothers after all." Erik spoke up even as the Confederate officers called out the orders to fall into formation. All around the Groetshven troops gathered and prepared to depart from the city where they would take up the march towards Istangrad where they would attempt to seize the capitol.

Travelling on their easterly course, the Groetshven forces spanned the distance over the course of a week or so- every day had seemingly blended into a single eternal cycle to the battle-weary troops. When they finally saw the Voskan fortress looming in the distance their commanding officers ordered them to pick up their pace. Rather than hearken at the thought of nearing the night's encampment, they collectively gave an exhausted sigh as they reluctantly trekked on at double speed. Twelve kilometers from the walled city of Istangrad, the officers finally gave the orders to stop and set up camp for the night prior to making a southerly the following morning. Tobias and Erik ate their rations alongside the remnants of their squad; there were only five original members besides themselves- nearly half had been killed or wounded over the course of the Groetshven campaign.

Erik chewed thoughtfully on his hardtack whilst observing Tobias as the artist drew a rough sketch of the scene around them. In his picture there were provisional tents obscured with dead branches and leaves for camouflage around the trees and thickets that dotted the rougher northern grasslands. Soldiers sat around munching on their rations under the starlit sky with the Voskan fortress of Stangrad looming ominously in the distance- a burning beacon in the night. Their squad was rather quiet and grim; the majority of their fellow countrymen had already experienced the loss of the close friends and relatives they'd started their deployment with. The remnants of the original squad were comprised of the sole survivor of what had been three peasant brothers, a drafted vagabond, a couple soldier's son's filling their father's boots, and a disgraced student.

"*Wie gehts*? I bet none of you thought we'd make it this far…" the former student chuckled uneasily, hoping to break the silence that hung over them

"My brothers used to joke with me about all the things we'd do after the war. I can still remember their laughter, the same way I remember their final moments. I've never truly felt *sehnsucht* until today." the lone brother replied rather listlessly as he stared off into the distance.

"If I had any, I'd bet money the orphan outlasts you schoolboy." the vagabond spoke up.

"That's wretched; he's not even orphaned!" one of the others spoke up, though the majority of their squad kept to themselves.

"So, have you drawn anything cheerful lately?" Erik spoke up suddenly, hoping to distract himself from the moment and interact with the last person he considered a friend in that place.

"I've never drawn anything cheerful in my life; I'm an artist. I just put what my mind shows me onto canvas." Tobias responded without a moment's hesitation.

"So that's it? You just draw death and despair now?" Erik scoffed.

"When have you ever seen me draw such things?" Tobias snapped, shoving his notebook into Erik's hands, demanding that he find an example therein.

"Alright, then explain this!" Erik snapped back, shoving the picture of Marc as he extended his hand out, grasping tufts of grass as he desperately tried to escape death in his dying breaths.

"That's our friend's final moments; fighting with all his life. It's a matter of perspective; you can call it sad and gloomy or you could see the strength and determination he displayed in his his fight for life."

CHAPTER SIXTEEN

NORTHERN GORGOVNA

Autumn, 2E9

Weeks had passed by since their desertion at the Battle of Stangrad, though still Alexei and his fellow surviving countrymen marched on, ever northward towards the safety of Alvaria outside the reach of Voskan control. Their officers led them onwards and offered them motivation- they were all equal now under the laws regarding desertion and their officers had earned their respect. Avoiding the Voskan cities, towns, and outposts that dotted the frigid northern highlands, the remnants of Stangrad marched along in hopes of reaching safe haven in Alvaria. It was the last pocket of land in Eastern Aerbon the remained free of Groetshven or Voskan control and was ruled by Lord Dragoş of House Matei and had been since before the Gorgon War.

"*Byt' ostorozhen*; there's a patrol ahead…" one of the officers warned, having spotted the small squad of four in the distance that appeared as a tan dot in the misty grey distance.

"There are too many of us to avoid their sight and besides; they've probably already spotted us." another spoke up in response. Sure enough, the patrol made their way towards the group and waved them down, signaling for their attention.

"*Privet* comrades! For what purpose do you march? It is clear by your clothes that you're battle-worn." the squad leader spoke up as the remaining commanding officers stepped forth to represent their soldiers.

"We march north to seek reinforcements. Stangrad is fallen and the Confederation of Groetshven marches upon the capitol as we speak. Time is of the essence comrades; go back to your post and spread the word." one of the officers spoke up without a moment's hesitation.

"*Cyka blyat*; those bastards… We'll spread the word and help as we're able. Go with all due haste" the squad-leader of the patrol swore, calling out his response as he turned and sprinted with his fellows back from whence they came to pass the message along.

"*Nikoim obrazom*; the truth really does set you free…" an officer laughed and a couple of soldiers shared in his mirth. Alexei breathed a sigh of relief; although brief, the situation had been tense for everyone involved and every man there was fully prepared to shoot the four man patrol dead should things have gone awry.

Continuing on their northerly course unopposed, the remnant host trekked along as quickly as they could before news of their desertion caught up to them. The land grew rougher and their path became more arduous the further north they progressed until finally they reached the rough mountains of the lands that served as a natural border between Gorgovna and Alvaria. Having no option but to dismount their horses, the officers dismounted their beasts and bid them farewell before allowing the soldiers to kill them to use for meat to keep themselves fed on the remainder of their journey. It was perfect timing as their rations were running low and the meat would last them enough to make the rest of their journey. Although none of the men took any joy from killing the horses, they rejoiced upon taking camp when they sank their teeth into the fresh meat after cooking it in the fire pit.

CHAPTER SEVENTEEN

NUREMBERG, GROETSHVEN

Autumn, 2E9

The Groetshven prison convoy drew to a stop outside the military checkpoint into Nuremberg Prison- formerly the town of Gorgorovna under the Voskan State. Commanding officers stepped forth to declare themselves and the caravans they led to the officers at the gate to see that their papers were in order. Once everything was accounted for, the caravan was granted entry and Petyr, alongside his fellow imprisoned Voskan kinsmen, were taken into the Confederate prison camp where they would be forced to do hard labour for the duration of their imprisonment. Upon their arrival in the prison camp, the occupants of the prison caravan were ordered to disembark and line themselves up for what the Confederate soldiers were calling their Assessment.

"*Achtung!*" a Groetshven commander shrieked as he approached, ordering the prisoners to attention. Petyr and a handful of the prisoners snapped to attention, standing upright and proper as if it had been their Voskan commanders ordering them. They were called forth and separated from the rest of the group before the Groetshven commander barked a second order- directed this time at his own me- demanding that they beat the insubordinate soldiers who refused his initial command. The prisoners attempted to defend themselves, though their pathetic attempts were futile; weakened by their starvation, the Voskan prisoners were no match for their Confederate captors.

The commander issued another order for his men to cease once he was fully satisfied, having relished in the brutality whilst the obedient Voskan prisoners watched the abuse of their fellow countrymen in horror. Calling them to attention a second time, the battered Voskan prisoners of war scrambled to their feet as quickly as they could lest they receive a second beating. Only a handful of soldiers refused the second time and so the Groetshven commander in charge spoke directly to one of the officers present.

"*Schaff sie weg.*" the officer nodded as he was given the orders, passing the command along to his men who proceeded to take the disobedient prisoners away.

"*Idi nakhuy izmennik.*" one of the prisoners spat at Petyr as he was escorted away; the same one that had done so aboard the caravan en route to the prison camp.

"*Proshchay neudachnik.*" Petyr replied with a bitter grin as he watched the prisoner's Groetshven escort shove the stock of his musket into the man's belly for his behaviour.

The men were taken away from the gathered crowd and escorted into the open area of the field where they were gathered. Once they'd taken their place, the Groetshven soldiers lined up whilst their commanding officer ordered the prisoners to do the same, and so they were executed by the Confederate firing squad. Once the soldiers were finished with the task they returned to await their next command whilst a prison crew took the corpses away under the watch of their own guards. Satisfied, the commander ordered the remaining prisoners to line up for their Selection, leaving the obedient one's to sit back and observe their fellows. They had been selected as prefects to watch over their fellow kinsmen whilst the rest had to survive the Selection in order to determine their role within the camp.

CHAPTER EIGHTEEN

CASTLE NACHT, ALVARIA

Autumn, 2E9

"For what purpose do you trespass upon these lands?" Dragoş addressed the entire host before him as if it were a singular entity rather than a group of individuals united as a whole.

"We are deserters of our army and we seek refuge in your lands." one of the officers came for, speaking for his countrymen.

"What concern is this of mine?" Dragoş laughed as he spoke; it was quite obvious that he had no interest in their plight.

"We're just conscripted soldiers; war is no concern of ours. We fight to survive in the hopes of going home- we'll fight for your cause if you help us with ours." Alexei blurted out, stepping forward as he addressed the lord directly.

"*Cine eşti tu?* Who are you to speak so boldly?" Dragoş replied to the young infantryman.

"Though you may not care to know, I am Alexei Rodionovna Ilyich; the eldest son of Aleksy Zuykov Ilyich." Alexei replied.

"So you would pledge yourself and your people to my cause without any knowledge of what that might entail?" Dragoş inquired. Alexei had managed to arouse the northern lord's interest.

"We're just soldiers; we follow orders and we fight for our lives- whatever that entails. We just want to go home, wherever that may be, whatever the price. We fight so that we won't have to fight anymore." Alexei replied.

"I'll give you peace, but it will cost you your souls; if you can part with those, I'll give you all that you desire…" Dragoş replied, though his words roused suspicion in the gathered Voskan deserters rather than comfort them.

So it was that Dragoş, Lord of Alvaria, gave the order to his men to take the deserters away and find them accommodations in the meantime whilst he figured out how to use them to his own advantage. The Alvarian lord withdrew from the courtyard and returned to his castle as the guards escorted the Voskan deserters away to take them into the town outside where they would receive housing from Nacht's inhabitants. Alexei followed his fellow countrymen as they allowed their escort to guide them along the town's narrow cobblestone streets towards the many humble abodes of the town's residents where they would be taking refuge. Each deserter was called forth as a pair of guards escorted each of them to their host's doorstep where the guards would proceed to knock, speak to the resident, and motion each of the Voskan men into their new accommodations.

Once he was settled into the house he'd been assigned, Alexei stretched and prepared himself to lie down even as a knock came at the door. The Alvarian man who owned the house turned to answer the door and was greeted by the pair of guards that had escorted Alexei to the residence and they explained they had a message for him. Calling Alexei to the door, the Alvarian man returned to his business in his own bedroom whilst the guards passed their message along to Alexei in the man's sitting room. They told him that Lord Dragoş wished to speak with him at the castle after midnight. Alexei thanked the men for delivering the request and bid them farewell to prepare his meeting with the Alvarian lord...

"So... Alexei Rodionovna Ilyich... you're an interesting one..." Dragoş stirred as Alexei entered Castle's Nacht throne room.

"*Vashe Vysokoprevoskhoditelstvo*; for what purpose do you summon me. My lord?" Alexei replied, formally addressing the lord in customary manner of his own people.

"*Nu este Vosia*; this isn't Voska, my friend. You need not address me in such a fashion." Dragoş replied before continuing, "You've disavowed yourself from your country and your people; I like that about you. You are your own person and I respect that; don't enslave yourself to the mortal world anymore."

"What do you mean?" Alexei was noticeably perplexed by the mysterious lord's words.

"For what purpose did you abandon your people and declare yourself and your countrymen free?" Dragoş replied, interested in the answer he would receive.

"We are just soldiers; the majority of us were serfs and peasants before that… If we had followed the demands of our liege and the officers who enact his will then we would have died defending a concept." Alexei gave his answer, staring into the face of the lord before him.

"Ah, yes; there you go! You chose to serve yourself rather than a… concept!" Dragoş laughed, "That is what I like to hear. The mortal world is beneath you and you saw firsthand the value of your life; so it was you who made the decision to see past the illusory man-made constructs of power to serve yourself and your kinsmen followed suite."

"What good is a pawn that frees itself from the game of its masters?" Alexei replied with a question of his own.

"There you go! This is the answer I seek for myself; what good are you and your kin to me? I can give you unfathomable power, but for what purpose? I wish to join in this game, but alas my own pawns are few and lacking the motivation to play that you display." Dragoş was full of mirth, those his words only continued to further perplex the young Voskan deserter.

"So what would you have us do, my lord?" Alexei replied.

"Life is binary; it is not what I would have you do, but what you would do for me. Join me, and I will show you things beyond your comprehension." Dragoş proffered Alexei a place by his side as he strode towards the balcony. Castle Nacht was built upon a cliff overlooking the town that had been built at the foot of his majestic fortress, and so the balcony gave them a beautiful panoramic view of the surroundings lands from where the castle sat atop the mountainous region. Alexei took in the view even as Dragoş took him by the shoulder, gripping him with inhuman strength and turning to face the lad even as he sank his teeth into Alexei's neck. The youth cried out in agony even as the Alvarian lord feasted upon his blood, feeling the life drain out of him as the blood poured down his neck and he was unable to resist as consciousness faded from him…

CHAPTER NINETEEN

ISTANGRAD, GORGOVNA

Autumn, 2E9

"This is it…" Tobias spoke up, staring at the horizon where the ominous capitol of Istangrad stood proud and tall.

"Can you believe it? We're nearly at the end of this wretched journey." Erik smirked as he cleaned his musket in preparation for what the officers were calling The Final Battle in their bloody war against the Voskan forces stationed in those lands.

"*Nein-* this is only the beginning." Tobias replied.

"Ach- for once can't you just be a little positive? You're always so gloomy; at least I try to maintain hope." Erik grimaced.

"Even the Sun has the Moon." Tobias chuckled, forcing a grin upon his friend's face. They enjoyed the remainder of the moment together in silence as they rode along in the wagons on the trek to the capitol. Tobias continued to sketch in his notebook as he rotated between pictures of his fellow squad-mates, the Iron Teeth Mountains that stretched across the horizon, and a couple pictures of the towns they'd conquered, filling in the details of each outline as he passed the time by. Erik observed him with some interest, though he kept to himself for the most part.

After some time had passed they were drawn out of their reverie when their commanders called them to disembark, ordering the host to continue the rest of the way on foot. They marched for a few hours before setting up a provisional camp on the outskirts of the capitol in the Iron Teeth Mountains to the south of the Voskan city. They would attack the city from the east, coming down from the mountains to seal off their escape route and drive them into a corner in their death march. Taking up the remainder of the journey at the break of dawn, the traversed the base of the mountain range on their northerly course as they drew nearer to the capitol by the hour until suddenly it was within their sight. Setting up a provisional camp in the safety of the rough and jagged mountain, a few of the officers ordered their companies to hold their position and gave them busy work whilst the rest of the host prepared themselves for the impending assault.

Following in formation with their squad, Tobias and Erik kept alert as they crept along, making their way towards the eastern outskirts of the capitol. The outer slums of the city were unprotected and provided the Groetshven troops with adequate cover to infiltrate the capitol where they would advance towards the ringed wall that surrounded the city centre of the capitol. As the soldiers marched through they ordered the Voskan peasantry and civilians into their houses as they passed through, stirring up fear and confusion in the streets as they continued onwards. Pushing forward, the Confederate soldiers made their way towards the high street where it transitioned from the Iron Highway and immediately took to cover as a Voskan patrol spotted them. Firing upon the Groetshven invaders, the patrol's squad leader called out for help from any nearby soldiers to help repel the attack, though there were far too many of the enemy troops to hold them off.

Gunning down the patrol and the handful of reinforcements that rushed to their call, Tobias, Erik, and the rest of their company continued to push on towards the outermost wall surrounding the city centre. Alerted by the sound of gunfire, more Voskan troops approached in an attempt to investigate the source of the disturbance. Tobias quickly reloaded his musket as he ran towards cover and jumped out to fire upon them as soon as his gun was ready. Erik took cover in an alleyway across the street and Tobias watched him follow suit as the Groetshven painter reloaded his musket to join in the third volley. The Confederate troops took turns firing in waves between the squads that comprised the advancing companies to lay down continuous suppressing fire on their Voskan enemies.

The Voskan forces fell back and sent a couple of the quicker youths amongst their ranks to run for assistance and alert the city to their plight. Aiming down the barrel of his musket, Tobias fired a shot that downed one such lad, watching the young soldier collapse as he himself ducked back into cover. A lead ball whizzed over his head where'd he'd just been standing a moment ago and he reloaded his musket to fire back on his attacker. One of his squad-mates dived into cover beside him before preparing to fire on the Voskan troops. Tobias took advantage of the volley to jump out of cover and sprint forward towards a market stall where he ducked down to reload after shooting down another musketeer.

"*Ikh slishkom mnogo!*" one of the Voskan soldiers called out, firing his musket before falling back as the Groetshven forces continued their advance.

"*Verpiss deine mutter*!" Erik shouted out at the Voskan soldier, shooting him dead before running forwards under the cover of another volley.

"*Otstupleniye*! There's too many of the, fall back!" a Voskan squad leader shouted, giving the order to retreat.

"The Tsar's orders are to fight to the last man- not a step backwards!" another officer replied. Tobias fired another round at the attacking Voskan troops as the squad leaders squabbled amongst themselves.

"*Cyka blyat*! If you want to die here then be my guest!" the first officer said, bidding the captain farewell as he fell back alongside his squad. A handful of Voskan soldiers stood their ground and continued to fire upon the advancing Confederate forces, providing suppressing fire to cover the retreat of their fellow countrymen. Tobias and his fellow squad-mates continued to advance until they were upon the outer wall of the city centre. The entrance was protected by a military checkpoint, though Voskan forces were already pouring out to stop their assault upon the capitol. Even as they approached cannon-fire erupted from the west and catapulted rocks and boulders began crashing down upon the city centre as the artillery support from Stangrad arrived and began their own assault.

The attack had taken Istangrad's defenders entirely by surprise and in the heat of the moment they were rendered totally discombobulated in the midst of the Confederate conquest. Falling back and taking refuge behind the protection of the outer wall, the Voskan defenders hunkered down and bolstered up their defences as they attempted to hold off the siege attempt. The Groetshven soldiers took refuge in the slums of the outer city and laid siege upon the capitol. So began the long and bloody battle for Istangrad- artillery constantly boomed as the western support rained down constant fire upon the city-centre. The infantry soldiers worked alongside the battering rams during the night to hammer away at the outer gate's defences under the cover of night whilst the Voskan troops fired upon them in an attempt to repel their attackers.

CHAPTER TWENTY

BAIA MARA, VOSKA

Winter, 2E9

First Marshal Dmitri Porfiry Yaroslavovich awaited his meeting with Vladyslav Vladimirovich-Ivanovna, the Tsar of Voska; smoking a pipe as he sipped his black tea. The officer was seated in the lobby of his own office in Baia Mara within the military complex. The complex was comprised of a series of blocs, including a university, training academy, barracks, headquarters, and arms manufacturing facility. His office was situated in the southwest wing on the seventh floor, giving him a perfect vantage point of Lake Giurgiu. At the present, however, he was seated in the lobby outside of his office, decorated by the four flags of Baia Mara, Voska, the Voskan Army, and the Tsar's family crest. It was an ornate room and he even had a young woman working for him as a receptionist. The room was just as decorated as one would expect for being the lobby of the military's board of directors; there were doors leading to the offices of the First Marshal, Second Marshal, and Third Marshal, as well as the General of the Infantry and the General of the Artillery*.

"Ah, Dmitri; *privet*? How have you been comrade?" Vladyslav greeted the commander of his army jovially as he entered the room.

---

*Formerly known as the General of the Cavalry in the First Era, prior to the invention of gunpowder.

"*Vashe Vysokoprevoskhoditelstvo**; it is good to see you! Things are not going so well in the West, I fear." the First Marshal nervously replied, shaking his leader's hand.

"So I've heard… The Confederation is implementing what they call a "lightning war" and their *Blitztruppen* are seemingly unstoppable with the combined advantage of range and guerrilla warfare. This is no news to me *Polkovnik*.ᶴ" the Tsar replied rather dismissively.

"So then what are you asking of me, *Vashe Vysokoprevoskhoditelstvo*?" Dmitri replied rather bewildered by the Tsar, though he was well-known for his eccentric and philosophical personality.

---

*Ваше Высокопревосходительство. Voskan; translates to "Your Highest Excellency. Used to formally address the Tsar of Voska.

ᶴ Voskan military rank, roughly corresponds to a colonel. In this context, the Tsar is subtly implying that the First Marshal was no more than a common general.

"It would seem quite clear, First Marshal, that you're a soldier first and foremost. What is it that you need of me?" the Tsar replied airily, obviously having lost his interest in the conversation.

"I... *Vashe... blyat...* We need twenty artillery companies, and at least an additional 50,000 men." Dmitri blurted out, overwhelmed by his anxiety and hoping beyond hope that the Tsar would thoughtlessly agree.

"*Cyka blyat Polkovnik*; what the fuck do you take me for? A common idiot? You can have fifty cannons and twenty thousand men to accompany them, or however many free men and serfs you can muster up on your own." the Tsar spun round on his heel and departed from that place, having concluded his business in that dull place. There were five cannons per artillery company and so the Tsar had effectively give Dmitri half of what he'd requested. It would still be a great asset to the war effort, though Dmitri had made the request in the hopes of maintaining a standing chance of going on the offensive rather than simply bolstering their defenses.

CHAPTER TWENTY-ONE

OUTSIDE MURMANSK, ALVARIAN BORDER

Winter, 2E9

"Ready yourselves." Alexei spoke up even as he braced himself. The marksmen positioned themselves whilst the infantrymen charged forth alongside the Alvarian troops that aided them. Under the cover of the starry night sky they were like blurry streaks that shot through the night as the stuck low to the ground in their forward charge.

"*Omoara-i pe toți!*" Dragoș hissed the order to his people even as he lunged at the first nightwatchman they stumbled upon whilst two of his men followed suite in taking victims of their own. Alexei and his company of marksmen observed the initial onslaught with interest from afar as they provided over-watch for the Alvarian vampires…

Awakening in a warm bed, Alexei took a moment to take in his surroundings as he stirred from what had seemed like an eternal slumber. He had no recollection of his past or even his own identity; a robed man stood over him patiently waiting at his bedside as the lad gathered himself together.

"Who are you; where am I?" were the first words out of Alexei's mouth as soon as he was sitting upright.

"I am Dragoş, Lord of the Vampires and Lord of Alvaria- the place in which you find yourself. In your past life you were known as Alexei, though I will allow you to keep it in this life as well." the lord spoke, revealing himself as he cast the hooded cloak aside, proffering his arm to his fresh and thirsty follower. Alexei unquestioningly took the lord's arm and sank his teeth into the flesh, greedily guzzling down the blood like a babe at the teat as the memories of his past life steadily came back to him...

"Ach- v...v...vampires!" a Voskan soldier called out as he witnessed his comrade fall to Dragoş' forces momentarily before a being dragged mercilessly to the ground himself.

"*Cyka blyat*, raise the alarm!" a Voskan officer called out as his attention was attracted to one of the several downed patrols. He fired a shot from his musket at the stooped head of a feeding vampire, blasting the creature of the night's head into an hundred pieces. Whistles screeched as the Voskan officers began waking their men, alerting them to the presence of attacking hostile forces. Alexei and his men picked off a handful of the Voskan infantrymen as they charged forth into the night as per the orders of their commanding officers. Some of the men dropped down into a prone position before firing off in the direction they assumed the attackers to be coming from whilst others sought cover or dodged the vampiric forces that assailed them. Dragoş and his followers sought out the commanding officers to destabilise the Voskan hierarchy and leave the troops leaderless whilst Alexei and his company of marksmen took down the attacking soldiers that posed a threat to their vampiric allies.

"There is no more need for bloodshed!" Alexei called out as Dragoş and his followers killed off the last of the Voskan officers in that small northern outpost.

"*Idi nakhuy izmennik*!" a soldier called out as his squad fired a volley in the direction of Alexei's voice.

"There are no gods, your commanding officers are dead, and you are no more than serfs, as am I, but I am free and we offer you each your own freedom." Alexei shouted in response; he and his men had ceased fire and many kept hidden under cover to shield themselves from any return fire whilst Alexei exposed himself to give his speech.

"*Blyat*... Fuck... Fuck you... You... You've sold your souls..." the soldier stammered as he dropped his musket and sank to his knees, seeing the futility of resistance though he was unable to accept the situation at hand.

CHAPTER TWENTY-TWO

ISTANGRAD, GORGOVNA

Winter, 2E9

"*Ausziehen*! Second, fourth, and fifth company- fall into formation!" Nils' captain called out, ordering their companies to follow his lead in a forward assault upon the besieged Voskan capitol. The cannons continued to boom as they fired upon the outer walls of the city centre, weakening Istangrad's defences as the main host of the Confederate Army continued to push deeper into the heart of the sprawling city. The Groetshven troops had already taken the outermost ring of the city centre and they'd been working their way towards the South Gate over the past week. The siege had been ongoing for nearly two and a half weeks and the Voskan forces remained undeterred by the efforts of the Confederate Army.

The First and Second Artillery Divisions had placed themselves strategically in the Southwestern district of the outer city whilst he Third, Fourth, and Fifth Artillery Divisions assailed the city from the North. Meanwhile in the Southeast Quarter of the inner-city, the main host of the Confederate Army assailed the Voskan forces head-on in the battle for the city centre. Nils and his company had been called to the frontlines to provide additional support for the main host in their endeavour. Escorting an explosives crew, a battering ram, and several siege engines, the host continued to attempt their advance upon the heart of the city centre. Nils fell into rank alongside Helmut and two other members of their squad; Elric Grimwald and Frederick Siegfried. Their squad was comprised of twelve lads, the whole company they served under consisting of 140 men.

Their secondary mission was to guide an artillery team comprised of three cannons and two catapults towards the eastern side of town within the outermost ring of the city centre. From there Nils and his fellow musketeers would advance to meet up with the frontline and push deeper into the capitol. The sounds of gunfire crackled from across the other side of the wall, though it was slightly muffled in comparison to the boom of the Confederate artillery. Nils captain shouted an order and all of his men picked up their pace as one body as they sprinted through the first gate towards the source of the gunfire. Up ahead they spotted their Groetshven countrymen and called out to them as they approached from behind.

A Voskan bullet whizzed by Nils' head and he ducked into cover just in time as another volley of enemy fire took down two of his squad-mates. Reloading his musket alongside Helmut and Frederick, he joined them as Elric took the opportunity to sprint ahead before taking his turn to fire and reload behind the safety of his provisional cover. Voskan gunfire pelted the Confederate troops in response whilst Nils and his squad-mates held to their positions, keeping their heads down lest an enemy shot put them down. Nils took advantage of the ensuing Groetshven volley to make another forward dash as Confederate musketeers fired upon the encroached Voskan soldiers guarding the checkpoint into inner city centre. Upon seizing the inner ring, all that would remain was the heart of the city- where the commander of Voska's army was most likely shitting himself.

"*Vorwärts*- kill the bastards!" Nil's captain shouted, ordering them to charge forwards even as they began falling into formation with the main host.

"*Scheiβe*, I was looking forwards to a break." Elric jokingly griped as he fired at one of the Voskan soldiers ahead.

"The sooner we take the city, the sooner we can all rest." another officer called out for all to hear as the other captains ordered their companies to advance.

"*Stoyat' na svoyem!*" a Voskan officer called out, firing down the narrow street as the Confederate troops pushed forward- onto the main road leading directly to the gate.

The Voskan troops fired openly without taking time to aim as the Groetshven troops charged forth in the hundreds, overwhelming the outer city centre's last line of defenders as they stormed the high street en masse. Nils took aim and shot down a Voskan infantryman even as the remnants of the defenders fired another volley at the rapidly approaching Confederate forces, downing nearly two dozen men as a result. It had no impact on the Groetshven soldiers as they continued to sprint without a moment's hesitation. Reloading as they ran, Nils and his fellow countrymen fired upon the Voskan troops relentlessly in waves as they stormed the city- their officers drew swords as they drew near and engages the remaining Voskan troops in melee combat.

More Voskan forces approached through the tunnel that served as the entrance into the inner city centre. The towering wall was roughly fifty meters tall and was all that remained of the original architecture comprising the Gorgon capitol. The entire city had been rebuilt in the aftermath of the Gorgon War and repopulated by Voskan peasants, soldiers, free men and Boyars. The Boyars mostly served as mayors in the newfound lands of the West whilst the peasants and soldiers laboured away at the reconstruction. For the impoverished peasants, this was the chance at a new life; they could make a new life for themselves in the western world and acquire their freedom as labourers. For the soldiers, they only served as a national duty, hoping to earn their freedom upon their return home. The Boyars ran the towns and cities that comprised the newly-acquired territory and served directly under their Tsar, ruling in the stead of their lord as well as paying the taxes of the country.

"*Scheiße!*" Helmut cried out, diverting Nils' attention momentarily as he turned in time to witness Elric collapse as he took a shot to the belly.

"We have to keep moving- *sich beeilen!*" Nils replied, ignoring the death of his friend as his mind only focused on the task at hand. Although his mind had shut down- leaving him in a dissociated state- he still felt the hate and anger that burned deep within him. This was what he relied on as the fuel to keep fighting. So it was that he sprinted forth with an extra burst of speed as he loaded another shot into his musket to kill those responsible and avenge his friend and all of their fallen kinsmen.

CHAPTER TWENTY-THREE

NUREMBERG, GROETSHVEN

Winter, 2E9

Life as a Groetshven prisoner of war was rough, and only made more difficult for Petyr by being an outcast amongst his own people. Calling him an *izmennik*, they ignored him and treated him the same as their oppressors to whom he answered. For this reason, the Groetshven officers had established separate living quarters for the subservient Voskan prisoners that they deemed worthy as prefects. They did this in an effort to protect them from the inevitable gang-beatings that occurred in the unsupervised communal areas. The prison prefects were responsible for supervising their fellow countrymen and reporting any suspicious or unauthorised activity to one of the several Groetshven officers that ran the prison camp. So it was that they had become hated by their peers for being the secret police that they were.

Having seen and taken note of this fact, the Groetshven officers personally oversaw the treatment of the *izmennik* prisoners, eating and talking with them, teaching them the Nardic language and learning Voskan in exchange. They even offered Groetshven citizenship to those whom served them in spying on and reporting their fellow prisoners. Petyr kept to himself mostly and rejected their offers to spy on his fellow prisoners, but he did offer to teach them Voskan. Although he refused to spy on his fellow countrymen, he wouldn't conspire against his oppressors either. They saw that he was a younger boy and so they did not pressure him, though when asked what he was doing in the military his response was simple.

"I'm just the son of a peasant; if you're at war with my country then your enemies are the Boyars. These people here are my friends, family, and neighbours. I don't want anything to happen to any of them; we just want to go home." Petyr told them.

"I understand your pain Petyr. These lands are ours, and your Boyars would seek to take them from us. My people have died for these lands and we earned them rightfully with our blood, and so we must take them back." the older captain present replied.

"So what does that mean for us?" Petyr inquired.

"Well, for now it means that this is your home- what it means at the end of it all... That depends on the outcome of this war, but I have no say in that; we're all just following our orders from higher powers." the officer answered rather vaguely, gesturing around at the prison complex they resided within.

"So have you got a family then?" Petyr asked after a brief pause.

"When I had first joined the army I was 17, that was after my father had died serving in The Gorgon War. The company I served were a reinforcing host sent to drive out the remaining forces in the land and then your people claimed the borders of the lands that we're presently seizing. I have no wife, no children, and I haven't seen what's left of my family since the day I joined. I love my people and this is my sacrifice." the officer replied, ending the conversation abruptly. Having concluded the discussion, the captain brought Petyr's attention to the matter at hand which was developing a Nardic to Voskan dictionary. The task was long and arduous, though it was significantly better than labouring in the fields outside with the general population of prisoners.

CHAPTER TWENTY-FOUR

EISENBERG, GROETSHVEN

Winter, 2E9

Having converted the Voskan troops stationed in Murmansk to their cause, the deserters made their way towards the former town of Ivanovo under the supervision of Alexei and Dragoş, aided his vampiric legion. From there they would travel onwards to Kosovo where Alexei would take a squad of his own and leave the main host under the rule of Dragoş to surround and seize the conquered capitol. There were rumours of a prison compound in the South where the Confederate forces were supposedly keeping prisoners of war- it was in Alexei's interests to check up on these rumours and see their validity for himself. Although Dragoş had seen fit to grant the gift of vampirism to Alexei, it had not been deemed necessary to bestow upon his fellow countrymen. So it was that Alexei had been given the blessing of the dead to help him guide the living.

Renaming the town of Ivanovo to Eisenberg, the Groetshven Army had left behind a small contingent to hold the town whilst they focused the majority of their attention on seizing the capitol. They left behind enough men to hold each of the towns and cities they'd conquered until the second wave was able to come through to populate the newly acquired territory and fortify their defences to repel any Voskan counter measures. As it was, the Confederate forces were not expecting an Alvarian assault from their northern neighbours and so they were taken completely unaware. The vampires charged ahead of their armed infantry support as they infiltrated the town and stuck to the shadows whilst they feasted upon the unsuspecting sentries and patrols that had been ordered to keep watch for the night.

"*Wach auf, wach auf*! Wake the fuck up- we're under attack!" a Groetshven soldier shrieked as he fled after witnessing his companion fall beside him, though he was tackled and devoured even as the words left his mouth. It was too late- another Groetshven soldier had raised the alarm, sacrificing his life in the process of blowing his horn as it alerted all of the vampires to his existence.

The vampires raced through the town devouring its inhabitants whilst the Voskan deserters stormed the outskirts, firing upon the Confederate troops as they sought to answer the call to arms after deploying from their barracks. Surrounded and overwhelmed, the majority of the Groetshven troops broke rank and attempted to flee from the monstrous creatures of the night that allied themselves with the soldiers of the Voskan Army. The deserters gunned down the retreating Confederate troops, leaving no survivors in their wake as they sought to liberate the city from Groetshven rule. Resistance was futile and so the Groetshven soldiers abandoned whatever hopes they had of defending Ivanovo from their demonic assailants as they fled for their lives to no avail. Alexei oversaw the eradication of their enemies with grim satisfaction as his company of musketeers made their way into the heart of the town centre.

Piling up the dead in the town square, Dragoş congratulated everyone present and thanked them for their efforts in the endeavour following their success. He proceeded to dismiss them to rest as the sunrise drew near, telling them that they would travel onwards to Kosovo before attacking the capitol with the full might of their unified forces.

"As if all of us together could hardly be considered a unified force against the full strength of the Groetshven Army in the capitol." one of Alexei's men griped.

"Don't worry comrade- we'll be focused on freeing the prisoners in Nuremberg." Alexei replied with cheerful irony.

"That's hardly any consolation! And if that's the case what does he mean by "unified forces" if we're going to split up?" the soldier replied, more disoriented and confused than he was at the start of the exchange.

"You think too much- just focus on the present." Alexei replied, brushing the conversation off as he lost interest, withdrawing to his own shelter to take refuge and rest through the day. The Alvarian Army made their moves by night and took refuge during the day to rest and the Voskan deserters followed suite whilst in their entourage.

"Easier said than done, comrade." the soldier sullenly replied as he sulked off towards his own barracks alongside his squad-mates.

"I'm a captain now." Alexei chuckled, having caught the soldier's mumbling and taking offence at the lacking use of his title when being addressed.

"*Da, Kapitan Izmennik.*" the soldier rebutted to the amusement of his peers.

"You wouldn't have said that to your captain in the Voskan Army..." Alexei stopped mid-stride to turn and face the rowdy soldier.

"*Da*, and this isn't the Voskan Army, *Kapitan Izmennik*." the soldier reminded him.

"Ah! That's right... How silly of me- it seems that it must have slipped my mind..." Alexei replied rather nonchalantly before lunging with all of his inhuman vampiric might. He tackled the soldier, appearing like a blurry streak of darkness to his fellow onlookers as he sacked the soldier before tearing out his throat and feasting on the corpse.

"Remember comrades…" Alexei spoke up slowly as he rose to his feet once his carnal craving for blood had been satisfied, "This isn't the Voskan Army. You take your orders from me. I take my orders from Dragoş himself, but it's none of your concern who I choose to follow as long as you're following me."

CHAPTER TWENTY-FIVE

ISTANGRAD, GORGOVNA

Winter, 2E9

"*Achtung!*" Nils shouted to his squad-mates as he ducked behind some cover- just in time as enemy gunfire whizzed by, pelting buildings, barrels, market stalls, and a handful of unfortunate Confederate troops.

"*Verpiss dich!*" Helmut shouted, popping out of cover to return fire upon the remaining Voskan troops that stood between them and the heart of Voska's western capitol.

"They will pay for the good men who died fighting for this accursed city!" their squad captain shouted.

"For Elric!" Frederic called out, cracking off a shot as he joined the Groetshven charge alongside his squad-mates.

"For Elric!" Nils and Helmut shouted in unison as they stormed the city centre, killing off what little was left of its defenders.

Pushing forward into the heart of the capitol, they tore down what was left the Voskan defenders, forcing them to cast down their weapons in surrender. Escorting the Voskan officers out from the citadel, the Confederate forces seized the city and rounded up the prisoners for shipment to the prison camps in Nuremberg. So it was that the Groetshven troops had proved victorious in their war against the Voskan Army, conquering the lands they'd lost in the aftermath of The Gorgon War…

"We did it Tobias!" a nearby soldier called out.

"*Ja*, it's finally over!" his fellow laughed in response.

"Get your rest boys- the war's not over yet. We have to plan our next move from here- enjoy the rest while you can." their captain replied, having overheard them. He dismissed them as he left to convene with the other officers.

"Hear that- it looks like our enemies still have some fight left in them, eh?" Helmut laughed, having overheard the conversation.

"Relax- we've got orders to stay behind and hold the city. We'd be lucky if we don't see any action here." their own squad leader replied.

"*Ja*, but we can still hope." Corporal Nils replied with a chuckle.

"*Ja*, because it's not as if gods would be of any help." their captain laughed before departing.

CHAPTER TWENTY-SIX

UZBEK, VOSKA

Spring, 2E10

The sun had finally begun to set as First Marshal Dmitri Porfiry and the host he led drew near their stopping point in the small rural town of Uzbek, deep in the heart of the Iron Teeth. They'd been marching for nearly seven weeks and they were just a little under a fortnight's march from the town of Uriya at the furthest reaches of Voska's western border in those mountains. His army was comprised of the fifty cannons and twenty thousand men that his glorious commander had seen fit to grant him, along with eight additional companies led by some of the local Boyars he'd convinced to aid him in his cause, promising the greedy noblemen plenty of fame and fortune over the course of the venture.

The total host he'd managed to amass amounted to 32,000 men and their morale was fairly decent given the circumstances. With the passage of the Winter and the onset of Spring, even the weather seemed to be on their side as the men enjoyed the more hospitable weather on their mountain trek. Although the Iron Highway kept them on track, shielded them from the weather's rougher elements, and provided them with shelter in the underground portions, it did little to protect them from the cold on the long stretches where they were exposed to the frigid winds and snow flurries that assailed them on the roughest portions of their journey. Their generous rations of vodka kept them warm however, and several hundred litres of the liquid had flowed over the course of their westward march.

"*Privet*!" one of the townsfolk called out, greeting the host as they approached the rural mountain town. The majority of the townsfolk had withdrawn indoors upon spotting the approaching army.

"I am First Marshal Dmitri Porfiry Yaroslavovich of the Voskan Army, serving directly under the Tsar himself. We require accommodations as they're able to be provided- the rest of the host can step up camp in the surrounding countryside." Dmitri said, casually waving around to motion the mountainous lands the inhabitants considered their farmlands.

"No- what are you doing! *Cyka blyat*- you'll ruin everything!" a farmer cried out, rushing forth even as the soldiers griped and groaned as they trampled the crops in their efforts to erect tents in the endeavour that comprised setting up camp. A Boyar casually shot the man dead as he angrily approached them and the rest of the townsfolk diverted their attention away from the troops.

"*Cyka*- where is that man's house? I'll make that my quarters, and his wife my mistress." the Boyar announced, following a local who guided him to the requested accommodations.

"*Blyat*- what a waste of a good man." Dmitri sighed as he turned away.

"At least his wife isn't going to waste." one of the men chuckled.

"What- what the fuck did you just say *suchka**?" Dmitri spun around on his heel, snapping off with a sudden rage.

"Nothing sir." the man replied abashedly.

"Oh- so you don't have balls; is that what you're telling me?" the First Marshal spat harshly.

*Suchka is Voskan for "little bitch", not to be mistaken with *cyka*.

"*Blyat*- I just figured at least his wife isn't going to waste… It's a shame I won't get to see her before I meet him…" the soldier replied as he glanced at a small crew of townsfolk busy at work taking the dead farmer's body away.

"Life is full of regrets." Dmitri replied thoughtfully as he shot the soldier, killing him before turning to face the rest of the troops that were present, "Let that be a lesson in the value of human life. I'm not particularly fond of you Boyars, but I expect better from my men. We are Voskans and we are equally as mortal as everything else- know your place and think before you act. The only thing the separates life from death is a fraction of a second- that's all it takes."

CHAPTER TWENTY-SEVEN

KOSOVO, GROETSHVEN

Winter, 2E10

The gunfire steadily began to cease as the Voskan deserters seized the small town of Kosovo with the help of the greater Alvaria host. Alexei relaxed as his men gathered around him, having secured the area. Piling the dead in the town centre, the Alvarian forces preoccupied themselves whilst Alexei gathered his men on the southern outskirts of the town. Congratulating his men on their victory, he told the battle-weary troops to prepare themselves for the trek to Nuremberg- ordering them to get as much rest as they could. Having concluded his address, Alexei sought out Dragoș to consult with him one final time before they parted ways.

"So what do you think of it all?" Dragoș inquired as Alexei approached, speaking in the language of the vampires.

"How do you mean?" Alexei replied, speaking in Alvarian to match his liege's desired dialect.

"What are your plans- when all of this is over?" Dragoș answered casually as he stared off into the distance, towards Istangrad.

"I just want to free my people, find my brother, and leave this war behind." Alexei responded without a moment's thought.

"You're people are already free under me- you're a vampire now. Don't forget that *prieten**." Dragoş rebutted, "Still, if you want to free the Nardic prisoners that's your choice."

"Why do you call them that?" Alexei inquired.

"Because that's what they are- or were, before they decided to take the name they claim now along with these lands that we presently find ourselves taking back." Dragoş replied with a sly chuckle.

"So what do you plan to do about them then?" Alexei rebutted with another inquiry.

---

*Alvarian for "friend."

"Ha- I was hoping that you would join me in ruling these lands once we take them back... I will return to my throne back in Alvaria-I have my own business to deal with besides the wars and plights of Man. I'd like to bestow you with these lands to deal with the affairs therein, but the choice is entirely yours." Dragoş replied, extending his offer.

"It truly is an honour, my lord, but I'm afraid I have to decline. I also have no interest in the wars or affairs of Man." Alexei replied, rejecting the invitation to rule.

"I understand, and I'm sorry to hear that it's your decision, but just know that the offer is still open should you change your mind." Dragoş concluded, bidding the Voskan deserter a good morning as the sunrise quickly approached following their night-time attack.

CHAPTER TWENTY-EIGHT

OUTSIDE URIYA, VOSKA

Spring, 2E10

"*Aussehen*- look up ahead!" Tobias heard one of the men call out from closer to the front of their formation. They were approaching a rural town cradled high up in those mountains further along the highway they traversed. It had been nearly three days since they'd escaped the seemingly never-ending tunnel that had comprised the first leg of their journey through the Iron Teeth and into Voska.

"*Vorsicht*! We have the element of surprise!" a Groetshven officer replied loud enough for his men to hear.

The host was comprised of roughly 8,000 men, the rest having been stationed in the conquered city of Istanberg. Reinforcements were being deployed to the frontlines as the second wave of Groetshven's army deployed to Gorgovna from the motherland. They were most likely passing through Gregov after having dropped off some of their men to aid in the reconstruction and protection of the town. In the meantime, the Groetshven leadership had seen fit to send their front-line forces over the Voskan border to bring the war to their doorstep in an effort to seize the town and hold it as a border-town.

"*Privet?*" one of the townsfolk greeted the invading host as they marched into the heart of the town, surrounding it with their troops.

"*Hallo freunde*! We are here on behalf of the Groetshven Confederation- we are here to liberate you from Voskan rule." the Groetshven commander announced, stepping forth to greet the villagers that were beginning to gather in the town centre. Upon hearing his announcement some of the townsfolk had begun to cheer and celebrate the news that they were being free of their servitude to the local Boyars.

As it was, the Boyars were only just receiving word of the Groetshven invasion- their messengers being the Confederate soldiers the captured them for shipment to Nuremberg as prisoners of war whilst their assets were seized in the name of the Confederacy. The local militia had surrendered themselves to the superiority of the Groetshven troops and they'd been conscripted into service in the Confederate Army upon yielding to the Groetshven forces.

"*Scheiβe*, that was easy enough!" Erik laughed as the pair stood by with their squad-mates.

"We're treading on deadly ground- I didn't think we stood a chance in Istangrad, but this is too easy… the calm before the storm…" Tobias replied uneasily.

"We won- now we're just securing the border. Maybe they'll send reinforcements when they don't hear back from their colonists, but they won't dare trespass upon this border once we turn them away." a nearby captain assured them, along with their fellow soldiers.

"Relax- this is our final destination! Once these lands are properly under the rule of the Confederation our work here will be done and those conscripted under the draft will be free to return to the civilian lives! This is it- stand your ground and fight for your freedom!" the leading commander called out for all to hear, taking a stand in the town centre, stepping down to the applause and celebratory cheer of his men.

CHAPTER TWENTY-NINE

NUREMBERG PRISON, GROETSHVEN

Spring, 2E10

"*Scheiße-* we're under attack!" a Confederate soldier cried out as he fell back from where he'd abandoned his post as the prison entrance.

"*Sich vorbereiten-* everyone to arms!" a Groetshven captain barked in response, leading a platoon of men towards the entry checkpoint where a group of Voskan troops were already swarming the handful of defenders that fell before them in their defence of the position. Petyr turned his head in anticipation as he sought to catch a glimpse of the affray whilst guards dragged him and the other *izmenniks* away.

"*Sich beeilen-* get fucking moving!" the Confederate officer barked, roughly shoving Petyr along with the heavy wood stock of his musket.

"*Izvinyayus-*" Petyr mindlessly apologised in Voskan as he sought to maintain his footing and continue moving along towards his lodgings where they were heading.

"What the fuck did you just say *ausländer*?" the officer shouted at him, kicking Petyr to the ground for his insolence.

"*Ich entschuldige mich für die unannehmlichkeiten!*" Petyr struggled to remember the phrase as he scrambling to regain his balance before receiving another beating at the hand of his oppressor in the heat of the moment.

"Get fucking moving- *sich beeilen du ficken scheiße!*" the officer shouted, turning to fire behind him as the Voskan assailants broke through their first line of defences.

"*Atakovat*, we fight for freedom!" Alexei shouted over the clamour and gunfire that filled the chaotic prison complex in the midst of the Voskan liberation. Prisoners shouted uproarious cries of joy upon the onset of the assault whilst guards were torn between responding to the assailing host and maintaining order amongst the inmates. Gunning down the Groetshven prison guards, the Voskan deserters kept them preoccupied whilst Alexei used his vampiric might to free the prisoners and horrifically slaughter anyone that stood against him. Guards fled before the gruesome vampire and his company of deserters whilst the former prisoners took up the arms of their dead captors to use against their remaining kinsmen.

"I'm sorry it has to end like this…" the Groetshven guard spoke somewhat mournfully as he turned to face the prisoners before him, withdrawing from the window where he'd been watching the raging battle outside.

"*Bitte*- please, you don't have to do this." Petyr begged the captain from where he stood with his fellow prisoners before a firing squad in their barracks.

"Silence *izmennik*; do you really want your last words to be a pathetic plea for your life? Sit still, be quiet, and be a man for once." one of his fellows reprimanded him, having accepted his own death as had the rest of those trapped in that room.

"*Feuer frei!*" the officer cried out, giving the order as his firing squad carried it out, blasting all of the Voskan prisoners before them into the Void…

"We did it! We really did it!" one of the Voskan deserters cried out in celebration of their victory as they rounded up the remnants of the surrendered Groetshven troops into a single mass before executing them- much to the shock of the Confederate survivors in their final moments.

"*Blyat cyka!*" a soldier exclaimed as he fell before a group of soldiers who fled from one of the barracks they'd holed up in before falling to the greater host of Voskans amassed in that complex.

Approaching the fallen soldier to investigate the building from whence the remnant troop of Confederates had been discovered, Alexei saw that they'd executed the Voskan prisoners that had originally inhabited the building. He looked away in disgust, but spotted something that caught his attention in the process. Returning his gaze to the pile of dead prisoners, Alexei saw his brother's face amongst them and felt his soul drain out from his body and spilled out into nonentity through the fabric of reality and into the void that it shrouded. Shrieking in total agony, Alexei sank to his knees as the reality of it all sank in and he felt a burning rage ignite deep within him, replacing his soul with the vengeful lust of hatred.

CHAPTER THIRTY

ISTANBURG, GROETSHVEN

Summer, 2E10

"Looks like the reinforcements are here ahead of schedule, eh?" Helmut spoke up as a host of Groetshven troops approached the capitol.

"They got here pretty quick." Frederick agreed as they stood watch over the southern entrance to the city.

"That's odd- they look pretty rough too, they must've encountered some trouble along the way..." Nils took note as the host drew nearer.

"*Wei gehts!*" their squad leader called out as the host came within range.

"*Omoara-i pe toți!*" their leader called out from amongst them as the mass of undead Groetshven troops fell upon their living kinsmen with all the vampiric might of the Alvarian forces they served.

"*Scheiße-* what the fuck!?!" Nils exclaimed as they fired upon the assailing undead army. One by one the Confederate troops that defended the southerly entrance to the former Gorgon capitol fell to the Alvarian vampires and their Groetshven converts as the Confederate soldiers fought to stand their ground.

"Fall back! Fall back- into the city!" Nils' captain cried out as a vampiric Confederate tackled Frederick to the ground- his death cry rang in Nils' ears as he turned and rand for his life whilst reinforcements rushed to investigate the source of the commotion.

"*Tot die tötten-* the dead have risen!" Helmut shrieked as he ran past the charging reinforcements in the opposing direction. The Confederate defenders fired fruitlessly upon the opposing vampiric masses as they dodged the lead projectiles to snatch up the helpless musketeers before feasting upon their bodies before the life drained from them.

Another wave of vampires approached from the South, joining into the affray as the vampires broke through the city's outer defences. The new attackers seemed to be foreigners from the North as far as Nils was able to determine from their attire, and they fought alongside the vampiric host of Confederate converts as they pushed the Confederate forces back, deeper into the city towards the inner ring wall.

"We can't let the city fall!" an officer cried out as he charged alongside his company of new arrivals, firing upon the advancing vampiric host in the midst of the Confederate retreat.

"*Verpiss dich-* run for your lives!" Nils' own captain cried out as he passed the man. All around Confederate soldiers were falling to the superior might of the vampires and resistance seemed futile.

CHAPTER THIRTY-ONE

GREGOV, GROETSHVEN

Summer, 2E10

Having left a couple companies behind to join the forces occupying Gregov, the host of Confederate reinforcements had departed from the town to continue on their northerly trek to the city of Kosovo where they would leave some more men on their journey to Istanberg to maintain a stranglehold over the eastern reaches of their Confederation. Lieutenant Hans Lindemann had joined the ranks of the reinforcements after being transferred from his post in Nuremberg to lead a division of his own after intercepting the host in Gregov. The host made its way steadily as they marched across the rolling plains that covered the expanse of land between Gregov and Kosovo, dotted with clusters of woods and smaller thickets of trees and other vegetation.

Lieutenant Hans had taken note that the reinforcements were armed with improved muskets, later finding that they had been manufactured in Rome based off the Groetshven design. The most notable difference between the Roman muskets and their Voskan/Groetshven-imitation counterparts was in the trigger*. Being higher quality than the Voskan muskets and their Groetshven replicas, the Confederate Army had invested in the Roman arms and began using it as the standard arm of their infantrymen in the Winter of 2E9, shortly after it's invention in the Summer of that same year.

*See FIREARMS in appendix.

As they approached the outskirts of Kosovo, the Confederate troops were greeted by gunfire, returning it with their superior Roman muskets. The improved arms were more accurate and powerful than Groetshven models they were adapted from, though their ammunition was slightly smaller than the Voskan weapons- the Roman muskets fired .72 calibre shots in comparison to the .69 and .75 lead balls of the Groetshven and Voskan muskets respectively. Hans also noticed that the Roman variants were also significantly lighter than the outdated Groetshven models. There were even some amongst the shipment of Roman muskets marked with the Confederate seal of Gewehrstadt's arms factory. It was known that the Groetshven Confederation had allied itself with the Roman Empire, but Hans hadn't realised that it entailed mutual production rights.

"*Aufladen*, attack!" Hans shouted to his men, ordering them to charge forth.

"*Für das wohl von die Kaiser*!*" the cavalry shouted as they charged forth ahead of Hans and his division of musketeers.

"That's going a bit far, but you get the idea men- let's go!" Hans shouted, following the cavalry's lead and mustering his men to join him.

*Groetshven. Loosely translates to "For the greater good of the Kaiser"

They assailed the city and its Voskan defenders, finding many of their own amongst the ranks of inhuman troops. Their opposition seemed immune to the bullets, though a handful of them had fallen to the Confederate marksmen. As the Groetshven host drew closer, they came to find that their adversaries were not mere mortals as the vampiric forces fell upon them. It was a total bloodbath as several Confederate soldiers fell for each vampire they killed*. Although they significantly outnumbered the Voskan troops numbering 45,000 strong, at least 15,000 men had given their lives to take those of the 4,000 vampires that had opposed them.

*Although vampires displayed inhuman power, they were at their weakest during the day, and so they proved more vulnerable to the bullets of the muskets- their strength and sight were significantly weaker in the direct sunlight, leading to the myths that it could kill them, although if they were in a severe state of blood-withdraw it could prove fatal.

CHAPTER THIRTY-TWO

CITY-STATE OF ISTANBUL

Summer, 2E10

"Our hope may be in the sewers!" one of the men suggested as the remnants of the Confederate soldiers took refuge within the safety of the city centre's inner wall.

"*Verpiss du und dein mütter-* of course our hopes have gone down the drains! If you have nothing better to do but state the obvious then put yourself to use!" a captain reprimanded the soldier harshly.

"*Nein-* what if we could use these sewers to our advantage and escape?" the soldier replied, desperate to explain himself.

"What-" the officer was dumbfounded by the idea.

"What would we do even if we did escape?" another captain joined them, seeing his fellow's inability to keep his own men in line.

"*Scheiße*, what's your plan? To die fighting this nightmare army of the dead?" Helmut laughed, chiming in.

"Those are the words of a deserter." the captain replied testily.

"Ah, I see-" the first captain interjected before continuing, "It would seem that Captain Heinrich is suggesting leading an attack against the enemy; he will need as many volunteers as he can get. As for the rest of you, I will be taking my orders from the only man present who seems to have any good ideas amongst us."

"*Verpiss du-* we're damned either way!" the second captain snapped, taking offence.

"So then now is the time where you must choose your death." his fellow laughed in response.

"Ah, so you're choosing a coward's death- I see." the second captain sneered mockingly.

"I'm choosing to take my chances in the hopes of living to see another day- I'll only take orders until they lead to my demise, that's where I'm taking my leave." the first captain rebutted, silencing his compatriot. So it was that the remnants of the Confederate host in that place gathered around to formulate a plan of escape. Although many would have to give their lives for it to have any hopes of success, it would at least ensure the survival of some of the men rather than the needless death of their entire force.

CHAPTER THIRTY-THREE

URIYA, IRON TEETH MOUNTAINS

Spring, 2E10

"*Atakovat*! Seize the village!" First Marshal Dmitri Porfiry Yaroslavovich shouted as the Voskan artillery boomed, firing upon the small mountain town from afar.

Charging forth, several companies of Voskan troops charged forward along the Iron Highway whilst the greater host had diverted from the road and scattered into the surrounding mountainous woodlands in an effort to reach around and flank the Confederate troops using the cover of the rough wooded terrain to their advantage.

"*Scheiße-* it's no use!" an officer cried out as he witnessed an artillery blast wipe out his entire squad in a single moment.

"*Verpiss dich*, fall back- there's too many of them!" another captain cried out, signalling the retreat.

"Are there none who will stand with me?" Erik cried out defiantly as he stood his ground, firing upon the advancing Voskan forces.

"Have you gone mad *freund*? There are too many to take them head-on!" Tobias cried out as he fired his own musket to cover the retreat, lingering as he hesitantly waited on his friend.

"All of our friends died fighting these bastards head-on; I won't join them with a gunshot-riddled back!" Erik rebutted as he downed another incoming Voskan infantryman.

"*Du bist verrückt*- you've lost your mind!" Tobias exclaimed, firing another shot off before falling back as he reloaded, watching as Erik also fired another volley with the retreating Confederates, standing his ground as the Voskan forces fell upon their position, encircling them from all sides.

"It's no use- resistance is futile!" the First Marshal shouted from afar as he approached upon horseback. Erik fired a shot that whizzed past Dmitri's head, though it embedded itself in an infantryman further back.

The Voskan forces continued to gun down the remaining resistance whilst Tobias and the remnant of the Confederate host attempted to fight their way out of their entrapment and flee back from whence they'd come. Erik continued to stand his ground even as the frontlines of the Voskan Army closed in upon him, executing him firing-squad style as they rushed him head-on- a squad comprised of fifteen men against him on his own. Tobias cried out as he watched Erik in his final moments, dropping his musket and sinking to his knees as he watched them kill his friend. Seeing the Groetshven painter give up hope, his kinsmen joined him in surrendering to the superior might of the Voskan forces and so they were taken as prisoners to be shipped off to Baia Mara.

CHAPTER THIRTY-FOUR

CITY-STATE OF STANGRAD

Autumn, 2E10

"*Scheiβe-* do you think it's going to be another bloodbath like Kosovo?" one of Hans men spoke up, seeking his opinion on what laid in wait for the host.

"I should hope not- otherwise our time in these lands would surely be at an end. These Voskan monstrosities are beyond the might of ordinary men- they've raised our own dead against us." Hans replied, voicing his honest thoughts on the subject.

They made their way into the fortified city without any trouble- to their dismay they found the entrance unmanned and the doors to the fortress wide open, though the walls were still in a state of disrepair in the aftermath of all the fighting they had been forced to bear witness to.

"*Hallo?Wei gehts!*" the commander of the host called out. His voice echoed off the ruinous remains of the city as it reverberated throughout the lifeless streets as they marched along.

"If you're Confederate we come in peace and if you're Voskan we apologise for trespassing!" a soldier shouted jokingly in response to the heavy silence that enveloped them. A couple men laughed at his joke whilst Hans let it slide rather than reprimand the soldier for his attempt at lightening the overall mood. Spreading out, the Groetshven troops searched the city for any signs of life or what could have led to the fortress' abandonment. As it was, they found nothing, delving deeper into the heart of the city even as the sun began to set. Suddenly a cry pierced the night, followed by the blast of a musket before another shriek injected fear into the hearts of every man present.

"*Scheiße*- this is how it ends!" a soldier shouted as he fired upon a lunging vampiric adversary. The bullet flew through the malefic monster as it latched on to him, tearing his jugular open as it sank its jaws into his neck.

"Stand your ground!" Hans shouted, blasting the creature's head with a shot from his own musket as two of his men followed suite. The monster toppled over as its head was blasted open, though the fresh human blood coursed through it and gave him ungodly power.

"*Toţi vei muri**." the vampire laughed as his head healed itself seemingly instantaneously as he returned to his feet, wiping the blood off his chin as he turned to face his attackers.

"*Feuer frei*! Let's kill these abominations!" Hans shouted as he and his men fired upon the monstrous beast in a twenty-three-man volley. The beast was blasted to pieces even as two more turned their attention to the victorious Confederate squad, lunging into the midst of the men and lashing out violently even as they reloaded.

"*Tot die tötten!*" one of the men cried out, inciting a chant from all the nearby soldiers in an effort to rally them as the vampires fell upon them.

"*Verpiss dich*- this Voskan devilry is too much!" another soldier called out as he fired his musket in an effort to cover his retreat- it was futile as a vampire swept down upon him, tackling the unfortunate Confederate musketeer to the ground and devouring him alive as he screamed in agonising pain and terror.

---

*Alvarian. Translates literally to, "You are all dead."

"We're totally exposed!" Hans shouted in desperation as he fell back, calling for his men to join him. Rushing for cover, they sought to evade the vampiric forces as the undead host began to gather en masse whilst the night continued to drag on. Descending upon the Groetshven troops in the heart of the town centre, it seemed as if the vampires were raining down upon them from the heavens above as they assailed the soldiers from all sides. The Confederate officers began calling for their troops to spread out and seek shelter in squads in an effort to wait out the attack until the safety of the sunrise signalled their salvation from the overwhelming vampiric ambush.

CHAPTER THIRTY-FIVE

ISTANBUL

Summer, 2E10

"Be on your guard- something is amiss!" the First Marshal called out as the Voskan host cautiously exited the mouth of the tunnel entrance to the Iron Highway, spreading out into the city of Istangrad outside. Not a soul could be spotted as far as they could see and it gave the city an eerie air in its abandoned state. Towards the south of the city they spotted a handful of retreating Groetshven troops, roughly 1,500 men or so.

"Halt! *Ostanovis gde ty!*" Dmitri barked at the Confederates that he assumed had been occupying the city prior to their arrival.

"So this is the mighty force that overthrew my men? You must be a mighty bunch." the First Marshal sneered as he addressed them whilst his men encircle the small contingent of Groetshven troops.

"Ha, don't be so cocky- there were more of us before those monsters came along." one of the few remaining Groetshven officers rebutted.

"*Jerundá*, what a load of bullshit- what is this you would have us believe about monsters?" Dmitri laughed, though more than a few a his men stirred uneasily.

"It's true- the dead have risen!" Helmut spoke up.

"*Ja*, we escaped through the sewers- they devoured all of our kinsmen." Nils chimed in.

"*Ja*! *Ja*, we thought this was your work until you lot stumbled along so obliviously into this ambush. Do yourselves a favour and go home, but either way leave us be- we want to live!" another soldier spoke directly to the First Marshall with a sense of urgency in his tone.

CHAPTER THIRTY-SIX

BAIA MARA, VOSKA

Autumn, 2E10

Over the course of his imprisonment it was noted that Tobias spent the entirety of it in isolation, tirelessly scribbling away in his notebook that the guards had allowed him to keep. His crazed fervour and dedication to his art intrigued his guards- they did not bother him or distract him, though their curiosity ate away at them as they wondered what it was that kept him so busy and took up all of his attention. Indeed, he hardly ate and his body began to with away from malnourishment as the days turned to weeks, yet still he dedicated himself to his art. After some time had passed he stopped answering to their knocks and his meals began piling up. At first the guards had thought nothing of it, peering in to find him slumped over the notebook in his usual corner, busy at work.

Finally, entering the room for a routine inspection, the prison warden held back a retch as the stench of death greeted him- flies buzzed around the corpse of the young Groetshven painter where he sat slumped over his sketchbook. Covering his face with a rag, the prison warden extracted the notebook from the corpse in its early stages of decay and departed from the cell, shutting the heavy iron door behind him before sealing it off to be cleaned out for future use. The guards crowded around as they all displayed an interest in what the notebook contained, pressuring the warden to share its contents with everyone present. Submitting to the unanimous request, he opened it up, flipping through the pages one by one as they showed the artist's life as he lived it through the pictures he'd captured with his mind's eye.

The initial drawings were of the Roman countryside and small towns that dotted Groetshven, as well as the cabin of a Confederate officer where the young painter was apparently riding along as a passenger. Continuing further they saw scenes of his training, his squad, their camps, portraits of individual squad-mates laughing and smiling as well as pictures where they posed with their muskets, grinning proudly as they looked onward or towards the sky. The pictures took a darker turn and became more gruesome as they depicted scenes of battle and portraits of his dying countrymen in their final moments, capturing the horrifying looks of agony upon their faces in brutal realism. The warden handed it over to one of the captains as he was forced to turn away, perturbed by the imagery he'd subjected himself to.

The captain continued to flip through the remainder of the pictures, displaying them for those who still desired to see more- a handful of guards had joined the warden in departing from the gathering to reflect on what they'd seen. The pictures continued to depict the death, destruction, and suffering of war and continued on to the capitol of Istangrad where Tobias had drawn the city as he saw it and also done a rendition of what he imagined the Tuhk of Istul must have looked like in all of it's grandeur- envisioning it as a majestic elvish citadel in its days of glory.Continuing further, the gather Voskan soldiers stared up the beautiful views of the mountains that the Iron Highway offered, recognising the town of Uriya in his artistic portrayal of it along with several portraits of its smiling townsfolk following the Groetshven occupation of the town.

From there the following pictures took another dark turn as they portrayed the death of his friend in a final stand against their men, his execution being the theme of several ensuing pictures. Finally they drew upon the end of his sketches, comprised predominantly of birds, flowers, and finally a portrait of himself, just as dead, listless, and malnourished in the picture as he was in the final moments leading up to his death. Although the photo-realistic self-portrait was unnerving enough on its own, even moreso were final three. The next one was the same picture, but his jaw was grotesquely dislocated as he held it in his hands, shrieking with bold black scribbles in the background. The following picture was the same, except that his skin was rotting and peeling off as he screamed in agonising pain. The final picture was a burning skull whose remaining flesh shrivelled up as the flames devoured it whilst the jaw was in the same fixed position as the previous portraits, leading them to believe that it was the final stage of his agonising demise.

CHAPTER THIRTY-SEVEN

CITY OF STANGRAD

Autumn, 2E10

"*Scheiße!*" a soldier cried out as he was dragged to the ground nearby Hans in the midst of the battle. Firing another shot from his musket as the Confederate soldiers sought cover to wait out the nightmarish attack until the sun's saving grace washed over them in a few hour's time.

"*Dein blut riechst so gut!*" one of the Confederate vampires called out mockingly to his former compatriots as he descended upon them in his Groetshven uniform.

"*Verpiss du und dein mütters!*" one of the Confederate troops called out, desperately firing alongside his squad-mates upon the monstrous beast in their midst.

"How could you betray us so-" another soldier rebutted in agony as the vampire tore his throat open with its claws. Grasping the victim's throat in his jaws, the vampire sank his teeth into the man's neck as the life steadily drained from him, temporarily sating the ravenous monster's bloodlust.

"*Scheiße-* there are too many of them!" one of the officers shouted as he reloaded his musket, covering the entrance to a factory as his men breached the building in an effort to get off the streets.

"Daybreak will soon be upon us!" Hans cried out in response, charging alongside the captain's men as they poured into the hopefully abandoned building.

"*Es ist sicher!*" a couple soldiers reported, having cleared the building in the squads that swept it in an effort to secure it.

"*Scheiße-* what the fuck are those monsters?" a sergeant swore.

"The Voskans have set demons loose upon us…" his fellow corporal replied.

"*Nein-* these things are beyond the evils of the Voskan Army… These lands were Gorgon before they were ever Groetshven or Voskan." an older captain spoke up.

"*Ja-* I still remember the Tar Beast…" Hans reminisced on his encounter with the colossal Gorgon monstrosity years ago during his time in the Nardic Army when they'd seized the Kingdom of Gilan from the elves that had populated it prior to the onset of the Second Era.

"My father told me that was a myth- nothing ever came of it and it's far too big to be hiding in the mountains." another soldier spoke up, laughing at Hans as a couple of his peers chuckled amongst themselves.

"Ha- your father wasn't there like the rest of us then… I still remember that day, as would any who were there. I was just a boy at the ripe age of fourteen- that was over ten years. Unless you can explain what I witnessed for what it was, then don't speak on the subject with the opinions of people who weren't even there." Hans rebutted.

"Ay- I remember you now. You lived down the street from me in Baiern… Hans wasn't it? I'd always fancied your mother Aeryn." the officer who'd held the door for him laughed, greeting him properly, "*Ich bin Todd, Vize-Feldwebel Todd Steine.*"

"Ah- yes, my mother had been very beautiful in her youth… She died a few years ago, back in 2E5- she had never taken my father's death well and grew very sick upon moving here. I haven't seen Frank since I left- he ran away after I'd left and no word has been heard since." Hans said reminiscently, catching up with the old hometown friend.

"*Ja-* I was just a little older than you too… I'd also wanted to avenge my father's death- I think that was the story with a lot of us back then…" Todd replied.

CHAPTER THIRTY-EIGHT

CITY OF ISTANBUL

Summer, 2E10

"Not so fast *suchka*- you're all coming with us!" Dmitri called out as the Groetshven remnants desperately sought to leave from that place.

"*Scheiße*- alright, but for fuck's sake, just get us out of here! We'll go with you freely, we just want to go!" Nils cried out in desperation to the amusement and unease of the surrounding Voskan troops.

"You really don't get it! There's a whole army of the dead here and when night falls- we're all dead!" Helmut chimed in, quickly changing the First Marshal's demeanour.

"*Chto*? What did you just say?" Dmitri's tone had become serious, urgent.

"What do you know of this?" Nils' captain inquired warily.

"*Blyat*- it can't be… Ten years ago when we'd laid claim to these lands we drove your people out, but they weren't the native inhabitants. There were disfigured beasts you'd been at work exterminating, but in the midst of your victory your people were assailed by an army of the dead- or undead. I led my men against them and drove the forces of evil out of this land- far north into the icy inhospitable reaches of the mountainous tundras that cover the lands past our furthest town of Murmansk." Dmitri spoke up to the shock of all who heard his tale.

"So then what do you suggest we do in the face of such an unstoppable evil?" one of the Confederate officers spoke up.

"How many of you were there that fell to these beasts in your defence of the city?" Dmitri answered the question with another.

"*Scheiße*- there were 12,000 of us left to defend this position- the rest went east to fend off those of you who stand before us undeterred by those whose fates you'd know better than us. Out of that 12,000 though- we are all that's left. The rest died providing us with the distraction that allowed us to escape via the sewers until the morning's light granted us the safety of travel that allowed you to catch us." the Groetshven officer replied.

"*Blyat*- so not only are they 10,000 stronger, but there were already enough of them to take down a host of 10,000 men? What is there to be done, when one is faced by death from all sides? Damned if we go back, damned if we stand our ground- it would just deem that we've been dealt the undesirable hand, but we'll just have to make the best with what we've got." Dmitri mused to himself aloud…

CHAPTER THIRTY-NINE

OUTSIDE ISTANBUL

Autumn, 2E10

"Prepare yourselves for the attack- *omoara-I pe toți*. Let's end this once and for all." Alexei said to his men as they prepared themselves to assail the capitol that laid ahead of them.

"We have the might of the dead god's army on our side- how can we be defeated?" one of the Voskan deserters laughed alongside a couple of his fellows. Although they were somewhat uneasy serving alongside a vampiric army, the fact that the nightmarish abominations were allied with them against their mutual enemies gave them all the confidence they needed to stand against any who opposed them.

"*Nu*. We fight for the Lord of Death- killer of the God of Death. He sacrificed himself to free us from the curse of our mortality, but instead he was damned to walk the earth with the gift that he's bestowed upon those who serve him." Alexei replied.

"I would rather keep my soul and retain my humanity than be cursed with that… *gift*, comrade." the former Voskan soldier replied, shivering uneasily at the thought of it.

"Lord Dragoş only bestows his curse upon the willing who take it for the gift that it is." Alexei replied.

"Oh, and what about them?" the soldier turned around to point to the host of vampiric Confederate converts that joined them from those that had been converted during the united Voskan-Vampire attack on Nuremberg.

"Those who oppose the will of Dragoş in their lifetime shall only fall to serve him in the afterlife." Alexei replied as a nearby Confederate vampire grinned at the uncomfortable soldier after his question had been answered, though it wasn't as much to his liking as he'd expected.

"So where do we stand when this is all over?" the soldier nervously inquired as his fellows looked to Alexei with a huge interest in the final answer.

"We will all be free of the chains of servitude that bind us under the rule of Dragoş." Alexei answered rather nonchalantly.

"And what does that mean for us?" the soldiers were incredulous at the vague response.

"As I've said before- those who oppose Dragoş will fall to serve him and he only bestows his gift upon the worthy and the willing. Those who should choose not to receive his blessing will be free to live their lives under his rule or go back to whatever place they consider to be their home." Alexei concluded, leaving the men to prepare themselves for the upcoming assault as soon as morning's light fell upon them.

CHAPTER FORTY

ISTANBUL

Autumn, 2E10

"Ha ha- by the grace of the sun, they're falling back!" Nils' captain cried out joyously as their vampiric assailants withdrew back into the inner safety of the city-centre to seek shelter from the sun that gave the soldiers their advantage in the open city streets.

"Let's hunt them down in their wretched hive!" Dmitri Porfiry Yaroslavovich cried out, leading his men towards the inner market district even as the vampiric masses fell back into the heart of the city centre where they convened like bees in a hive during the day.

"*Ja*, let's finish this once and for all!" Helmut shouted as he joined the men that rallied around the First Marshal as he led the spontaneous assault. Even as the remnants of the united host of Voskans and Confederates swarmed together in their efforts to assail the vampires in their provisional base, they were flanked from behind by newly-arrived Voskan deserters and former prisoners of Nuremberg who beset them from the south of the city. The newcomers forced the original host of Voskans and Confederates under the rule of First Marshal Yaroslavovich to retreat deeper into the city whilst leaving behind a sizeable contingent to cover their rear whilst they pushed on.

"*Scheiße-* and now a new contender joins the battle!?!" Nils exclaimed with a groan as he lingered behind to aid his fellows in holding off the new attack as the sun began to shine down upon them.

"*Das ist gut!*" Helmut laughed in response as he bid his friend farewell, continuing along with the First Marshal's men in storming the vampiric nest, "I was worried I'd have too much leftover ammunition when we get through with the demons!"

"*Viel glück mein freunde!*" a nearby Confederate officer called out as he fired off a shot, covering Nils during his reload as he joined in the effort to hold off the incoming band of Voskan deserters and former prisoners.

The newcomers pushed them back, forcing the first line of defenders of the rear guard to withdraw within the safety of the market's inner wall from where they'd been standing their ground on streets of the outer city. Meanwhile the First Marshal guided his men comprising the greater host as they pushed deeper into the heart of the city on the hunt for the vampiric masses that convened in the heart of the capitol within the reconstructed citadel in the centre. The sun rose to its peak even as they crossed the entrance leading into the innermost ring of the city centre and Dmitri continued to push his men to exert whatever energy they had left in the last-ditch effort to eradicate their unholy enemies before the sunset damned them all…

"It sounds like those men are putting up a good fight- who would have thought that they'd be able to see eye-to-eye to stand their own against us." a vampire mused aloud as Alexei guided them through the reconstructed sewage system of Istul, updated by the Voskans after having restored and improved the city since the days of its orcish occupation.

"It's as they say- *the enemy of my enemy is my friend*, eh?" Alexei replied as they continued to creep along.

"It's no matter; united they stand and united they will fall- we have the Lord of Death on our side." the vampire replied as they returned their attention to positioning themselves in preparation for the evening that was quickly approaching. Alexei's thoughts drifted to his lord, holed up in the capitol's citadel in the heart of the city centre. *Sunset is not far away- don't let them catch you yet*, Alexei thought to himself as he worried for the vampiric overlord whilst the remnants of Voska's mighty army hunted him down.

CHAPTER FORTY-ONE

ISTANBUL

Autumn, 2E10

"*Atakovat*- attack now, it's our only hope!" Dmitri shrieked the final order as the Citadel of Istangrad loomed towering over them- the host was upon its doorstep and they charged through the entrance even as their rear guard caught up to them, falling back from the vampires and their humanoid deserter allies that chased after them in the midst of the evening's onset.

"*Scheiße*, so this is how it ends!" Helmut cried out as he joined his fellows in storming the citadel that stretched out to reach the heavens- as had its predecessor before it. Vampires wrapped themselves around the towering walls that comprised the central lobby of the colossal building. The room spanned twenty feet tall and was shrouded in darkness as all light was blocked out by heavy curtains shrouding the tall windows that faced out to give a majestic view of the city streets where it rested in the heart of the capitol. Men had begun firing haphazardly without bothering to aim as the vampires descended upon them in the midst of their breach.

"You are not alone *freund*!" Nils called out, saving Helmut's life as he blasted a lunging vampire that had attempted to snatch him up.

"*Mein freund*! It is better to die by your side than these Voskan mutts!" Helmut laughed as they joined together to face the vampiric forces that assailed them.

"But better that you die by the hand of a Voskan mutt!" Alexei hissed from behind as he seized the Confederate soldier up by the nape of his neck before flinging him with inhuman strength.

"Helmut!" Nils cried out as he fired his musket at the monster responsible. Alexei swatter the musket aside, laughing as his own vampiric host swarmed the few remaining forces that assailed the citadel even as Dragoş' own vampiric host held their own against the breaching attackers.

"*Sufletul tău aparține acum lui Dragoș.*" Alexei hissed, sinking his teeth into Nil's throat as he devoured the Groetshven soldier, draining him of his life…

"So it is done." Dragoș acknowledged in the aftermath of the battle.

"Is it truly?" Alexei rebutted inquisitively whilst the majority of the host busied themselves about cleaning up the wreckage.

"*Da*, this is it. I have no plans for conquest- I don't even want these new lands; Alvaria is enough to manage. You can have this newfound state- let this be the bridge between the lands of the dead and the living. Those who do not wish to live amongst our kind can rule themselves in the southern lands bordering the Confederation." Dragoș replied without much thought.

"And everyone will just agree to that? Have you already spoken to the rulers of the armies we just defeated then? Surely it isn't over- not yet at least!" Alexei exclaimed incredulously.

"Ah, none of that is my concern. I've already expressed my will- now it is up to my followers to see it enacted. You know what happens to those who defy my will; our neighbours can either bend to it or break before it." Dragoş concluded, dismissing himself from Alexei's presence, having nothing more to say on the matter.

EPILOGUE

Following the conclusion of the Siege of Istanbul and the eradication of the united Groetshven and Voskan forces, Lord Dragoş bestowed the newly-founded nation of Ishtan to Alexei Ilyich to rule on his behalf as an ally of the Kingdom of Alvaria. It acted as a buffer-state between the vampiric kingdom in the North and the newly founded Kingdom of Gregovia in the South where the remnants of the Voskan men and those amongst the Voskan vampiric converts had decided to reside for the remainder of their days. Having managed to maintain their hold over Stuttgart until the saving grace of the sun's first light, Lieutenant Hands and the Confederate forces therein had secured the Confederations western border between Alvaria and the newly-founded nations of Ishtan and Gregovia.

Voska acknowledged their defeat at the hands of the Aerbonean vampires, though Vladyslav Vladimirovich-Ivanovna sent his own emissaries to relay the sole condition of their surrender being the placement of their own border patrol at the entry checkpoint to the Iron Highway in Istanbul, establishing a Voskan Embassy in the city- the first in all of Aerbon. He'd also shown an interest in the paintings of the late Tobias Schumacher, confiscating them from the Baia Mara prison camp to display in a museum he erected in the heart of the Voskan capitol's city centre in honour of the deceased Confederate prisoner. He dubbed the gallery "The Iron Heart" and displayed all of Tobias' war-themed sketches, paintings, and portraits whilst scrapping the more pleasant landscapes of Rome and his homeland. The paintings would go on to become highly prized and coveted international treasures later in the history of their world after Vladyslav's passing and Tobias would go on to become known as one of the most world-renowned painters in history- his most famous being the final depictions of himself in "The Shades of Loss."

FIREARMS

EARLY VOSKAN MUSKET

YEAR: 1E172 .75CAL

RANGE: 30M WEIGHT:12KG

IMPROVED VOSKAN MUSKET

YEAR:1E196 .75CAL

RANGE: 50M WEIGHT:10.5KG

GROETSHVEN MUSKET

YEAR: 2E5 .69CAL

RANGE:67M

WEIGHT: 9.5KG

IMPROVED ROMAN MUSKET

YEAR: 2E9 .72CAL

RANGE:70M

WEIGHT: 7.5KG

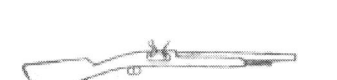

IMPROVED VOSKAN MUSKET

YEAR: 2E10 .75CAL

RANGE:65M

WEIGHT: 9KG

TERRITORIAL MAP OF SOUTHEAST AERBON

Made in the USA
Lexington, KY
26 November 2019